Antônio De Salles, Ph.D. lives in Brazil. Fascinated with the brain function during medical school, he learned how to improve its function at the Medical College of Virginia, Harvard University, and Umea University in Sweden. He became a world renown neurosurgeon, and neuroscientist becoming an Emeritus Professor at UCLA. He writes to bring awareness of state-of-the-art brain surgery. His novel *Why Fly over the Cuckoo's Nest?Psychosurgery in my Brain Please*, already a success in four languages, is here titled *The Brain of the Player*. The reader leisurely learns the intricacies of the brain and the ethical woes of its modification. Resilience through love, science and loyalty bring the reader to the acumen achieved by a dedicated wife, scientist, and mother.

Antônio De Salles

The Player's Brain

Love and Soccer

AUSTIN MACAULEY PUBLISHERS®
LONDON * CAMBRIDGE * NEW YORK * SHARJAH

Ordering Information
Quantity sales: Special discounts are available on quantity purchases by corporations, associations, and others. For details, contact the publisher at the address below.

Publisher's Cataloging-in-Publication data
De Salles, Antônio
The Player's Brain

ISBN 9781638292210 (Paperback)
ISBN 9781638292227 (Hardback)
ISBN 9781638293910 (ePub e-book)
ISBN 9781638293903 (Audiobook)

Library of Congress Control Number: 2024908579

www.austinmacauley.com/us

First Published 2024
Austin Macauley Publishers LLC
40 Wall Street, 33rd Floor, Suite 3302
New York, NY 10005
USA

mail-usa@austinmacauley.com
+1 (646) 5125767

First and foremost, I acknowledge my parents, both of whom were dedicated writers. Certainly, this is where my writing genes are from. Mom assigned me essays during school holidays, training my mind for storytelling and inspiring me to use time during my work vacations to write as a hobby. My wife, Alessandra Gorgulho, was the first reader of this novel. She encouraged the writing chapter by chapter and agreed to share our honeymoon with my lonely pastime. Out of their love for family, Gilka De Salles, Luzita De Salles and Marina Carneiro made the effort during vacation to read this story, which is written in a language that is foreign for them. They all encouraged me with their positive assessments and critiques. I also want to acknowledge Ana Gorgulho, who gave loving support to my son and daughters, and freed up my time to make my hobby possible. Several close friends had the patience to read through this manuscript and suggest structural improvements for my second language writing. I cannot offer enough thanks to Edward Mitchell, Sebastião Eurico de Melo-Souza, Harvey Bennet, Donald Becker, Goran Lacan, Patrick Kelly, Marwan Hariz, and Raul Marino. Lyn Rothman in London was available when I most needed a friend and was a major force once the manuscript was ready for outside eyes. She introduced me to Glenn Berenbeim and enticed him to read the story as a possible basis for a screen play. His enthusiasm brought his best friend and my editor, now long-distance cyber-close friend, Julia Hays, who dedicated hours and hours to revising my writing for a native English-speaking reader. Lyn again brought professional storytellers to my life when she suggested I join the master art lessons of Donald Freed, and subsequently brought Kate Johnson on board as a movie producer. These gifted collaborators showed me that in my naiveté, I was trying to achieve something way over my head. Finally, I thank my medical and scientific teachers and collaborators who, together with my trusting patients, provided me with the vision and knowledge to write on this subject. And, as I am now writing this acknowledgment in Liverpool, UK, I will paraphrase the Beatles, "I got by with the huge help of my friends…" friends mentioned as well as those not mentioned here and finished the job!

Table of Contents

Preface

Countless intelligent lives are condemned to remain separated from the main flow of society. Families lose their loved ones from their homes. Prisons are full of violent murderers that could be controlled with proper medical attention. The author has been the victim of a patient assault when he was a neurosurgery resident. Such episodes are common, occurring more frequently than advertised. Only when they lead to major tragedies are they reported in the media. Health professionals lose their lives in the name of treating patients that are not properly controlled by medications. Laws and societal restrictions hinder doctor's actions to help patients and protect themselves. These restrictions need to be revised in face of the explosion of effective medical technology available in the dawn of this century.

Recently a prominent psychiatrist and world-renowned scientist lost his life in his private office while consulting on a mentally ill patient. This writing is a tribute to health professionals that have lost their lives caring for violent psychiatric patients.

Chapter 1
Jill

Jill Riderhiem was observing the fight of a group of monkeys at the university's primate behavior research center. Some animals would leave hurt from this major war-like mess. These fights would sporadically happen, almost seasonally. After these episodes, the animals would become peaceful and go about their normal playful, feeding and sexual behavior, even among the ones that seemingly were enemies in the fight. Few would go to a corner of the colony enclosed area and appear sad.

It was difficult for Jill to understand what actually had transpired among the animals. What was the meaning of that whole commotion? She visited the colony to observe the animals just for enjoyment. The animals' behavior was curious and entertaining to her. Now, however, she was starting to observe them as part of her work as a Neuroscientist.

Jill had just started her undergraduate degree in neuroscience at the University of California in Los Angeles (UCLA). A petite, attractive 18-year-old Chinese American girl, Jill was a 'straight A' student with aspirations to become a medical doctor. She was taking one-month elective studies as a laboratory technician at the department of molecular pharmacology. She was fascinated by the intricacies of the brain pathways. She selected an elective in a laboratory studying means to control addiction and violent behavior.

Her sweetheart since junior high school, Charles Morales, had incredible rage attacks against schoolmates during sports. This aroused her interested in functions of the brain related to behavioral patterns. She loved Charles and admired his abilities as an athlete and as a student. She wanted to understand his behavior at those moments that he demonstrated lack of self-control and so much power. She decided to dedicate her studies to the understanding of brain function in a quest to help Charles. Specifically to prevent what would trigger his sudden rage attack.

Her first contact with behavioral science was in a high school project when she had the opportunity to spend part of her summer vacation observing how rats would learn to negotiate complicated mazes. She became amazed on how these animals would learn fast the intricacies of the maze to reach their prize. She enjoyed the quiet time observing the animals and the challenge of understanding them. She was also an animal lover.

Jill was raised by Swedish adoptive parents, the Riderhiems. She was adopted when she was a toddler. The Riderhiems brought her from the province of Anhui, in rural China, to San Diego. Girls were frequently taken for adoption in rural China because their natural parents abandoned then when they were born. The 'one child per family' law, in a culture where males were valued more than females, generated such aberration. Families preferred to abandon their female offspring for another chance to have a boy. The orphanages were crowded with little girls in rural China. Toddler girls, similar to what happened with Jill, would become immediately attached to couples that would give them even minimal attention. Jill clinched to the Riderhiems when they met her at 18 months of age. Jill became the life's reason for this already mature and dedicated couple, tired of infertility clinics.

The Riderhiems owned a pet store in San Diego. Jill grew up caring for animals. She helped her adoptive parents in the store. This environment taught her interest and kindness to animals. Moreover, it gave her a strict discipline.

Throughout her life, until she left home for college, she worked in the pet shop with the well-established routines of grooming and feeding the animals.

These acquired skills would help Jill in her quest. She was in the colony at this time not to amuse herself but trying to find a monkey that her mentor, Dr. Mallory, had assigned to her observation. The monkey number 956789, which she finally identified as one of the participants in the fight, had left the fight with a large scratch on his back and sat sad close to the colony's fence. She immediately gave it the nickname of Fred because of his strong features and offered him a banana. He grabbed it and ran away. Now that she had successfully identified Fred, her subject, she was ready to follow Dr. Mallory's instructions—first acquire the animal's trust to proceed with the planned experimental protocol.

Chapter 2
Jill and Charles

Rage had again taken the best out of Charles Morales. He came home after a fight at school during a soccer game. He received a red card for punching the referee who called him for a penalty against the other team's goalkeeper. Nineteen and athletic, Charles was the striker of the soccer team at the University of California in San Diego. Volatile, fast and secure in his moves, Charles acquired the respect of his peers and teachers. He became the sports hero of the college in his freshman year after taking the soccer team to the championship.

However, during the games, Charles was frequently confrontational with the referees and the opposing players. These impulses were mostly controlled by Bryan Cole, the team's coach. Despite minor disagreements Charles occasionally had with his teammates, his coach instilled friendship, respect and loyalty among players. They were a tight bunch, and most of the time Charles' teammates tolerated his tantrums to achieve the team unity preached by Coach Cole.

Tired after the exhausting game, Charles opened a bottle of Gatorade and sat in front of the TV of his home. He put on his favorite movie, *Casablanca*. Since his childhood, watching romantic movies was the best way Charles found to calm down after his fits of rage. His mother kept cartoons and love stories that were soothing to him around the house. She kept away any videos containing violence or crime. Charles would get excited and aggressive when he watched them. When he was 11 years old, he broke one of the neighbor's son's front teeth with a punch after watching one of Claude Van Damme's movies.

Charles' temper was well known in the neighborhood and at school; all knew not to disagree with him. However, he was not a bully. He was actually sweet and sensitive to others' needs; he just could not take confrontation well. It would always end up in violence. As a result, after graduating from high school, his mother sent him to college in his hometown, San Diego, to keep him close to her and continue to protect him from major problems, as she had done his entire life.

Near the end of the movie, Charles started to long for Jill. Charles loved Jill and admired her intelligence and discipline toward her studies. Besides being a great athlete, Charles was also a successful student with an interest in mathematics. Their relationship had led him to consider the field of Biophysics for his career. When he was not occupied by his soccer endeavors with his best friend since childhood Roberto Hernandez, he spent time helping Roberto with his math. Roberto had difficulty with his studies. Charles dedication to sports, school, his friend Roberto and the sweetness of his girlfriend kept him out of trouble during his teens. Their families protected him from any form of confrontation and encouraged Charles' and Jill's relationship. Now that Jill had started college in Los Angeles, Charles missed her terribly.

As 'The End' flashed across the TV screen, he had decided. He would visit Jill in Los Angeles that evening. It was only two and a half hours from San Diego. He would leave home at 5 PM, have dinner with her and take her to a movie. Since it was Friday, he would spend the weekend with her and return Sunday afternoon to be at school on Monday. Charles told his mother his plans and borrowed her car for the weekend.

Charles' mother was a nurse in a psychiatric hospital. When Charles was a toddler, she understood that she needed to learn to control his aggressive behavior to help her son through life. Charles' father, Mr. Morales, taught mathematics at University of California in San Diego. Although dedicated to his education, he was unable to control Charles' rage episodes. A mild Spanish American man, Mr. Morales himself could have an explosive temper when enraged. He did not accept his son's inability to handle confrontation with ease, as he saw his own mirror image in Charles. He let his wife deal with Charles' temper and manners, dedicating his time with Charles to sports and support of his academic endeavors. Charles did not have siblings; the love of his parents led him successfully through his childhood and teen years.

It was already 5 PM when Charles left for Los Angeles. Soft piano music playing in his iPod got him through the traffic from San Diego to Los Angeles. The sunset on the Pacific Ocean during the trip only made Charles' longing for Jill more intense. When he arrived in Westwood, it was almost dark, the sun had slipped into the sea. He had bought roses from a Mexican guy at the corner of Wilshire and Veteran Avenue. Jill was waiting with a candlelight dinner ready. She was beautiful, with a low cut white dress and long hair falling over her chest. She was all that Charles was longing for. When she saw the roses, tears came to her eyes. He lifted her in the air and said, "I love you. You look perfect!"

"I think you were just lonely there," she whispered.

"Yes, I was. I needed you so much today. I couldn't stay home without seeing you." He turned away and sank into her couch.

"I am glad you came," said Jill.

"I had a rough day at the soccer field."

"Tell me what happened."

"I got mad against the referee, you know. I punched him."

"Wow! I'm sorry, dear."

"I just can't take unfairness. Coach Cole came through again and calmed me down. Then, I got a red card and we lost, one to zero. I went home depressed, angry, and ashamed of myself." He looked up, "and needing your calming effect on me."

"Dinner is ready," she said and guided him toward the table.

Sitting across the table, he looked deep into her eyes and said, "Jill, I wish I could be with you all the time. You bring out the best in me. I love you so much."

"I love you too," she said. She held his hand and continued, "I also wanted you here with me. I had a long and interesting day in the monkeys' colony at the university. Tomorrow, I will introduce you to my new friend, Fred."

"It's great to be here, but who is Fred?" said Charles, worried.

"He's my monkey at the colony, you will love him. We will have a wonderful weekend. I just have to check Fred for half an hour tomorrow and on Sunday; otherwise, we will have the whole weekend for ourselves."

They sat and talked through dinner. She was excited about the research she was observing. Using primates, her mentor was studying community behavior of animals affected by different addictive drugs. She described how monkeys would prefer a 'screwdriver' to plain orange juice. Animals would soon become addicted to vodka, always choosing the alcoholic drink over any other. She was fascinated with how fast the animals became addicted and how aggressive they would become when they did not have access to alcohol. Other drugs were also being tested in the laboratory; however she was in charge of only the alcoholic monkeys.

She told that Dr. Hillary, a neurosurgeon, worked in the same laboratory and was interested in pure aggressive behavior. Experiments were ongoing to define areas of the brain that could be addressed to control rage episodes in the monkey without modifying their cognitive abilities and their interactions with the colony. Many times aggressive behavior gave them high ranking in the monkey-organized community. The challenge was to find a way to control an animal's aggressive behavior and still maintain its rank in the group. Dr. Hillary was studying functional images of their brains obtained with modern radiological techniques. Jill was fascinated by Dr. Hillary's findings and his scientific enthusiasm. During her conversations with him in the laboratory, Jill had acquired knowledge that would take her years of reading to grasp.

Charlie was listening attentively and interrupted, worried, "Who is this interesting Dr. Hillary, Jill?"

"Charlie, don't be silly, he is a professor of neurosurgery, could be my father."

Jill continued describing to Charles the brain pathways that were being studied in an attempt to control addictive and aggressive behavior. She talked about the millions of cells involved in the drug-seeking behavior circuitry and the repercussions of the lack of them. Charles was very attentive to her descriptions; especially interesting to him was the circuitry and how to control mathematically this complex computer system. They finished dinner, and Jill let Charles pick the movie.

***

They went to see a light love story and walked home holding hands. Charles was a romantic; he loved the part where the girl said to the guy how much she enjoyed tangling her hands in his hair and leaning her face to his chest. Jill agreed and stopped suddenly. Charles was 6 feet tall; Jill's head fitted perfectly to the height of his chest when they embraced. As she was talking, he felt very close to her. She placed her arms under his arms and ran her hands on his hair; pulled his head down toward her and kissed him deeply. Charles felt her closeness and his love for her. Full of desire, they rushed home.

***

The studio that Jill was renting for the summer from a professor in sabbatical was decorated in a French style. There was a divan at the entrance hall with a vase of fern close to it. The streetlight coming through the window gave the appearance of a moonlit room. Her white dress was slightly glowing, reflecting pale light that enhanced the dark color of her skin. Her long hair loosely draped over her shoulders, accentuated the prominence of her breasts. The dress, the draping dark hair and her delicate chin framed the valley between. He lowered his head and kissed her chin, then her chest and arranged her hair over her shoulders. Slowly caressing her neck with his lips, he lowered his head toward her breasts. She shivered and extended her neck, letting her hair fall back, offering him her blossom.

Gently, he undid the string laces of her silk dress, slipping it to the floor. He rested his head over her chest. She urged to have him inside her and moaned her love and her desire. He caressed her nipples and her bellybutton with his lips and gently exposed her completely. He brought her head up and kissed her mouth, feeling her intense love. After the passionate kiss, she undid his shirt and touched her breasts to his chest. He could not contain his desire. He lifted her, laid her in the divan and kneeled down on the floor, caressing her thighs and her knees with his lips, kissing her legs softly while she declared his love for him and moaned the intense desired that had completely overtaken her. She reached for him, undid his belt, opened his trousers and felt his strong and pulsating readiness. She caressed him, hastily undressed him and gently guided him over her.

He tenderly entered her at the same time that he touched his lips around her dark and aroused nipples. She held him tightly and gave rhythm to their love while her nails softly scratched his back. Shivering after seconds of this initial matching, he slowed their rhythm to a halt and felt her warmth and the overwhelming passionate pressure in his chest, uttering how intensely he loved her. He glanced at her face, noticing that her dark brown eyes were larger than usual, bright and wet, letting tears run over her love-flushed face.

He asked, "Am I hurting you?"

She replied, "I am so happy that I could not contain my tears."

She intensified slowly the rhythm of their becoming one body, building up to their ecstasy. They remained embraced as one being, enjoying the tenderness, the closeness and the complete marriage of their souls. They knew their destiny was linked forever.

As they rested in their embrace, Charles dreamed of his future life with her. Jill had an instinctive tenderness and complete dedication to him. She knew of Charles' rage attacks and the danger that this posed to others and to her. She felt the resolute strength she had to complement Charles' life and the ability to help him to overcome his anger episodes. She knew that he would need her through the confrontations of life. She had observed his episodes of rage at school; his power at those moments attracted her at the same time that it frightened her. She hoped that her love and her studies would suffice to build a happy life with him. Her youth, her love for him and her penchant for difficult challenges gave her the confidence to decide to spend her life with him.

That night, they slept in each other's arms.

She woke up late in the morning after that wonderful night. Charles was still asleep at her side. She woke him up with a soft kiss and rushed him out of the door to the university primate colony. She had to be at the animal colony to feed and observe the behavior of her subject.

Chapter 3
Jill and Charles and Fred

At the university colony, the animals lived largely free in a huge space enclosed by chain link fence encompassing a small lake and scattered large trees. The ambiance was created to mimic the animals' habitat as closely as possible. The setting was designed to fulfill all the animals' needs, letting them interact naturally and organize themselves in a societal fashion. The scientists would introduce the experimental drug or paradigm to an animal or group of animals without disturbing the established social order. For example, one animal would be trained on a task or given a study drug. Then it would be reintroduced to the colony and its adjustment to the environment would be recorded. Any change in the social order would be observed and corrected either with a drug, removal of a drug or a behavior modification training session.

Jill was observing how the alcoholic monkey was faring in the colony. She had been noticing that initially it was very aggressive and got into a lot of trouble with its mates. As she always provided it with the vodka it craved, over time it became docile and remained in a corner enclosure, always waiting for her in the same spot where she deposited the vodka with orange juice through a small window in the chain link fence. It had no interest in the females and avoided confrontation with the males. She recorded these observations meticulously on her protocol sheet, as her mentor had instructed her.

She was enjoying her task as a behavioral scientist; the greenery, the sound of the water cascading into the artificial lake, and the playful young animals gave her a peaceful feeling.

While she was working with Fred, Charles sat in the grass and observed the careful way she talked with the monkey, her consistence of movements not to scare him and the avid desire of the animal for the 'screwdriver' drink.

When she finished her work, she sat close to Charles, held his hand, and said: "I like this job, it is so interesting."

They continue enjoying the observation of the animals playing and their time together. Jill told Charles interesting aspects of the monkeys' life she had learned since she started coming to the colony.

This species of monkey, the Vervet, had an intriguing social order. The most aggressive male would intimidate his peers and become the leader and call the attention of the females to him. However, this was not enough to gain his mate. The female monkeys would bunch together into a fierce attack on the dominant male, beating him up heavily. If he could take the physical abuse and accept to be physically dominated by them, he would obtain their sexual favors and be the chosen mate.

This was an interesting natural selection behavior, because the best fit male to father their children, as judged by the females, was the one that could be aggressive when needed but also able to have complete control of himself in order to achieve his pressing instinctive goal. This ability gave the male monkey the leadership in the colony. He could physically protect the females yet allow them to dominate him at their will.

Jill was fascinated by this social order. She was observing how the alcohol addiction had completely destroyed her subject's desire to fit into this unique social paradigm. When she failed to give him the alcoholic drink, he would become extremely aggressive and start fighting with the males; however, he had no interest in the females. He would definitely not let them abuse him physically and would actually become aggressive toward them, since they were disturbing his quest to fulfill his addiction, in total abandonment of his mating instinct.

Jill, in her early scientific observation experience, was already making the parallel of this animal's behavior with the human situation. Here she had her loving Charles, an incredible stud, intelligent and sweet with her and his family, who had difficulty fitting in the societal order due to his inability to control his aggressive behavior. As the possibility of a fight was presented to him, he embraced it with an overwhelming instinctive and addictive impulse. She started to wonder how to manipulate her laboratory animal to control his withdrawal aggression and still maintain his ability to compete for the leadership of the colony and attract his female mates.

She started to care deeply for this animal; as she met him every day and gave him his vodka, he became more and more endearing to her. These wild animals would not become close to humans easily, yet the subject that she was now calling Fred was turning completely dependent on her supplying him alcohol. He would not survive in the colony without it; the other males would destroy him if he became aggressive. The alcohol allowed him to be depressed and uninterested in the colony. However, he needed more and more of it to keep calm. She knew from the human alcoholics that he would live a shorter life if he continued to be addicted to alcohol. He would eventually develop a liver failure and perish. It was now time to objectively study his brain circuitry and chemical changes generated by the alcohol.

The experiment with Fred would evaluate different computer-generated images of his brain's functional areas, and focus on both chemical activity and structure in these segments. Once early images had been obtained, Fred would be progressively desensitized and weaned from his addiction, so that he could reenter his normal life within the colony. Comparison of the images before, during, and after the addiction should yield a tremendous amount of information on the chemical and electrical effects, as well as the enduring consequences, of alcohol addiction. This was a very ambitious experimental protocol, because the functional image had to show cerebral metabolic changes during the animal's aggressive behavior. To obtain imaging of the animal's brain during its aggressive behavior was considered virtually impossible. All these computerized imaging acquisitions require a resting subject.

Positron Emission Tomography (PET) could provide the functional images, and Magnetoencephalography (MEG) could measure the electrical variations in the brain during the periods of changing behavior. The acquired digital data could be normalized into structural images of the brain obtained with Magnetic Resonance Image (MRI). These overwhelming complex data sets could be handled by smart software developed by a German company (BrainLab) that was already being used in the human clinical setting to diagnose and treat brain tumors.

The UCLA laboratory in which Jill was working specialized in the development of molecular markers of brain function. These markers were fast decaying radioactive isotopes constructed in a cyclotron and rapidly injected in the animal's blood stream during the behavior modifications. They would be taken by cells in the areas of the brain active during the behavior and be detected by the PET. The MEG could readily correlate the neurochemical changes detected by the PET with the electrical changes. These momentary changes in the brain could be mapped with micro precision in a high resolution MRI. This data could then be paralleled to the human brain for development of medical and surgical therapies.

The main challenge was injecting the molecular radioactive markers into the animal's blood stream at the precise moment the rage attack was initiating. Then, after the injection, promptly anesthetize the animal to have him placed inside of the PET scanner quietly for a precise imaging acquisition. Jill had spent so much time with Fred, her experimental animal, that she believed she could accomplish this task. That Sunday morning she explained to Charles her plan of action. During the next month she would gain Fred's confidence to allow her to place a secure intravenous (IV) and an intra-arterial (IA) catheter in exchange for his daily drink.

Once the IV and IA were secured, she would withhold the alcohol. At the moment his aggression started to build up, she would inject the markers IA and seconds later, necessary for the markers to circulate and be captured in the brain cells, she would inject the anesthetic agent IV. The animal would fall asleep and she would immediately place him inside the PET machine in the laboratory. This had to be precisely timed with the blood circulation through the brain to capture the molecular changes at the very moment the rage episode built up, identifying the specific site of the brain responsible for the behavior. This was important because this very site could offer the opportunity to control the rage episode with either electrical or chemical interventions. Although easily describable, this was a daunting task.

After describing all her plans, Jill, who was now laying on the grass with her head in Charles' lap, asked, "Well Charlie, what do you think?"

Charles kissed her forehead, mesmerized by her enthusiasm and creativity. He understood the challenge ahead of Jill. He ran his hand in her hair, looked at her and said, "If you can make Fred love you like I do, he will allow you to do anything to him. Just use your gentleness; I bet you will gain his confidence."

"I'll miss you up here by myself. I'll put all my energy and love to gain Fred's love and confidence."

"Jill, count on me! Let me know how I can help. It will be a great excuse to drive up here and see you," whispered Charles, kissing her lips softly.

Time had passed without notice. They were so relaxed together they forgot that Charlie had to drive back to San Diego. It was already 3 PM; they had spent the whole day so far with Fred. They sat holding hands in the grass outside the fence observing Fred and the playful monkeys in the trees and the small lake. Each ate only a half of an egg sandwich that Jill had prepared as a snack and enjoyed the peaceful setting and their closeness. Charles had to go to school the next morning. They had planned to see a movie that afternoon, but they ran out of time. Fred had entertained them longer than they expected.

They walked down to Westwood Village, to the Starbuck's coffee shop for a quick bite and a strong coffee. Charles would hit Sunday afternoon traffic and had to remain awake. He was estimating four hours' driving to arrive in Del Mar, just outside of San Diego, where his parents had their house. It was hard to say goodbye. Charles and Jill had possibly the happiest weekend of their lives. It took him more than one hour to finally kiss her goodbye and release from her tight embrace. It was so wonderful to love her.

***

He entered the 405 Freeway in a daze. Jill would not leave his mind. He was sexually aroused and could not let it go until he was close to the Los Angeles airport, already 45 minutes into the Sunday evening traffic. The freeway was packed with those driving into Los Angeles and the business travelers going to the airport. Charles was already exhausted from the bumper-to-bumper driving when the traffic eased up slightly and he picked up speed. A few miles down, a pickup truck suddenly crossed the outside of the car pool lane, grazing Charles' car on the side. Charles became completely enraged. He sped up and cut off the pickup truck, squeezing it against the concrete divider of the freeway. The cars came to a complete stop in a huge traffic jam.

Charles left his car and went directly to the pickup's driver's window. He started punching the driver. Blood splashed from the driver's face covering the front window of the pickup truck. Charles' hands and shirt were soaked with blood when several drivers ran out of their cars and held Charles while someone called 911. The police came and took Charles to jail.

The pickup driver was an illegal immigrant and was under the influence of alcohol. He had only few cuts and bruises on his face. He did not press charges of physical assault against Charles. It was proved that Charles was not under the influence of alcohol or any drugs. He was detained until his parents came and paid a steep fine. Charles had his driver's license confiscated. The lawyer the Morales contracted was able to clear him out of much complication with the law. The judge ordered him to perform community work and psychological help for anger management.

***

He missed school for a few days. His mother took him to his psychiatrist. Charles was placed on medication, but his parents knew he would not comply with it. Under medication, Charles would lose his quickness. He had tried it before several times, he turned into a poor soccer player, and was slow and sleepy at school. His grades deteriorated to a point that he hated himself.

His parents had a long conversation with him.

"Charlie, it is OK for you not to take the medication, but we don't want you driving alone to Los Angeles to see Jill anymore," said his mother.

"Mom, I need to see her, I love her. I may even transfer to UCLA to finish college," said Charles.

"We will figure out a way for you to get were you need to go accompanied by someone. This way you don't get into trouble," said his mother.

"It's not reasonable for you or Dad drive me around. It won't be nice to always have someone with me when I want to spend time with Jill," answered Charles.

"We will figure things out. Jill can come and Roberto can also drive you up there," said his mother.

Charles looked depressed but accepted the idea for now. He called Jill that night. She promised she would come to see him at least twice a week. She would finish volunteering at the cardiac catheter laboratory, get onto the freeway in the evening and arrive in Del Mar for dinner. They would have dinner together and alternate sleeping either in his or her parents' home. She would head back to Los Angeles the next morning before there was traffic and would arrive at UCLA to start work in the morning.

***

It was during this drive back and forth from Del Mar to Los Angeles that Jill listened to the unabridged recording of 'One Flew Over the Cuckoo's Nest' written by Ken Kesey. The neurosurgery professor working in the laboratory to develop surgery to control aggressive behavior suggested that she read it to enhance her understanding on the intricacies and social repercussions of behavior modification surgery.

Chapter 4
Charles and Roberto

As Charles was not allowed to drive, Roberto Hernandez became a constant presence in his life. Roberto was his soccer and school buddy. Playing as a midfielder, he was frequently serving Charles perfect passes that Charles was quick to convert into beautiful goals. They played very closely; Roberto maintained himself a few steps behind Charles. When he served a pass to Charles, he always prepared to take the rebound or continue the pass exchange with Charles. This close proximity was important in order for Roberto to keep an eye on Charles' reactions during the game and take advantage of Charles fast moves and rebounds to score. Many times Roberto prevented Charles from hitting someone during the game.

Charles would never commit a penalty on purpose. He was a very fair player, actually a gentleman on the field. He could not, however, tolerate an unfair play. Coach Cole instructed Roberto to stop Charles when he got out of control. This symbiotic relationship was advantageous for both. They were complementary in soccer, and in exchange for Roberto's help to control his rage, Charles would help Roberto in his academic work.

Roberto was a short and strong Mexican American not very good-looking fellow who had played organized soccer in Southern California since early childhood. Mr. Hernandez, his father, had played professional soccer in Mexico before immigrating to United States. He taught Roberto his position. Roberto became a calm and precise midfielder. He could analyze the game, judge the violent players and keep them away from Charles as much as possible. He frequently advised Charles to stay away from the unfair players, as he could quickly single them out. However this was not always possible. Also, because of Charles' quick moves and high speed, defenders' only option was to stop him from behind, frequently leading to penalties that gave his team free goal kicks. Roberto had a very strong and precise kick, converting a high percentage of these direct kicks into goals. They complemented each other perfectly in the field.

Their friendship went beyond the soccer field, however. Roberto wanted to be an architect, but he had difficulty in mathematics. They took courses together and Charles spent hours explaining concepts to Roberto. Charles was patient and an outstanding teacher, on this he had inherited his Mr. Morales talent. He had a clear understanding of mathematics thanks to his father giving him a solid foundation. Charles' gratitude for Roberto's dedication and protection showed in his desire to make Roberto successful in his academic aspirations.

Roberto did not have a girlfriend and when Jill was not in San Diego, he and Charles spent all their free hours together. Roberto was his true best friend. Charles confided to Roberto his deepest feelings. Charles described in detail his built up anger and his inability to control himself. He confessed to him his horror after his aggressions and the guilty feeling he carried in the aftermath of the episodes. A profound wish to apologize and the embarrassment that he felt had isolated him from other people throughout his life. That is why Charles had such a small circle of relationships, his parents, Jill and her family and Roberto's family.

Although Roberto sympathized with Charles' suffering, he did not know what to do to help him psychologically. This was a major vacuum in their relationship; Roberto felt that he was not capable to fulfill Charles' friendship needs. On one occasion, he confided to Jill his frustration of not being able to console Charles in his moments of depression.

When Charles was feeling inadequate, Roberto would cheer him up saying how lucky he was for being so smart, the soccer star of the school and for enjoying Jill's love. Charles agreed but he could not pull himself out of the depression for days. These depression episodes usually came after periods of rage as if his brain was completely depleted of energy. The depression would persist until his brain was recharged.

Heavy physical exercise and time spent with Jill were the best treatment for his depression. Roberto started to drive Charles up to Los Angeles to see Jill during the weekends. They would spend wonderful times together. Jill had acquired a special affection for the UCLA sculpture garden. She would prepare a picnic basket and they would spend whole afternoons sitting in the grass studying, observing the squirrels and talking about science, mathematics and soccer. During these peaceful conversations, Jill aroused Charles' and Roberto's interest in her experiments. She had the ability to entice an audience to her ideas with her eloquent descriptions and interpretations of Fred's shifts in mood. The parallel between Charles and Fred's behavior fascinated Roberto. He expressed to Charles his desire to help Jill on her experiments.

Jill asked Roberto and Charles to help her to design a cage for Fred that would allow her to record Magneto Encephalography (MEG) during his periods of rage and depression. This cage should also allow them to record the level of Fred's activity and at the same time isolate the experiment from electrical noise in the room. The animal's activity was a good measure of its level of depression. The deeper the depression, the less he moved around the cage. His movements were to be counted and recorded by a computer system attached to the cage. Graphs of his level of activity were to be generated hourly by a statistical software package.

Roberto and Charles took the task of constructing this cage to heart. Roberto managed electrical circuits very well, as Mr. Hernandez was an electrician. This was the profession he embraced when he immigrated to San Diego from Mexico City. Roberto helped his father at work while he was growing up. These skills became handy for the design and construction of the cage. Charles was a computer expert and developed all the recording capabilities of Fred's new home.

One weekend, Roberto and Charles drove from San Diego to Los Angeles bringing the cage that Jill had commissioned. She commemorated the event by cooking dinner for them and treating them to a movie in Westwood that night. The next day, early in the morning they went to the monkey colony to introduce Fred to his new home. Fred had to be transported from the colony to the UCLA laboratories for the imaging portion of the experiments. Roberto had designed the cage to allow Jill to restrain Fred when needed for imaging and medication administration. The walls of the cage would move in, tightening the space to an extent that Fred could not move. Jill discovered that tightening his living space was a good way to increase the frequency of Fred's rage attacks, allowing her to collect valuable data in a shorter period of time than at the colony.

That weekend, Jill, Charles and Roberto spent all their time making sure that all the components of the cage worked properly. They barely had time for meals. Sunday evening Roberto and Charles wished good luck to Jill and left for San Diego.

Charles felt very secure during this period of his life. Roberto's presence and Jill's love almost completely abolished his periods of depression and his rage attacks. He became extremely productive at school and decided that he would try for a doctorate degree in bioengineering at UCLA. Charles enjoyed the thought process he went through to develop Fred's cage. He liked the creative challenge. He could see himself isolated in a laboratory solving problems. It would be a secure and sheltered job, free of contact with people that could irritate him. Now starting his second year in college, he also was initiating his plans to marry Jill. He had already talked Roberto into being his best man and suggested that he should also try a graduate degree after college.

Roberto knew his own limitations and given the influence of his father he was more inclined to try hard to become a professional soccer player. He enjoyed soccer and it would fulfill his father's dream. He was having his studies supported by a soccer scholarship; Mr. Morales was making the needed contacts with agents and the professional soccer coaches to help Roberto find a professional soccer opportunity.

Roberto's partnership with Charles in the soccer field had helped immensely his recognition as a star player in the midfield. The constant penalties against his team that Charles attracted gave Roberto the opportunity to convert many free kicks into goals. The free kicks opportunities gave Roberto a unique sense of security as a soccer player. This kept him among the highest scorers in the majority of the tournaments. He and Charles frequently competed for the most valuable player in the tournaments. Both their soccer talents and their close friendship were well known by the coaches of the professional soccer teams in Southern California; sooner or later they would be invited to play professional soccer.

Charles' parents, however, felt that professional soccer was not for him. College soccer was different from professional soccer. Also there was no guarantee that Roberto would always be playing close to Charles. They knew Charles would not be able to handle the pressures of the professional competition. Sooner or later he would get into a major fight, with unknown consequences. They were in favor of Charles' marriage to Jill and his idea of settling into a scientific career. Charles also knew that this was the best course for him. He was making up his mind to talk to Jill's parents about his marriage intentions. He had however a sense of friendship with Roberto and did not want to let Roberto down in his aspirations. Charles understood well the importance of their partnership in the soccer field to assure Roberto's success.

Mr. Hernandez, however, was pushing Charles to enter professional soccer together with Roberto; he knew that his son would have better chances if he played side by side with Charles. All contacts had been already worked out for them to be invited to try for the major Southern California soccer team, the Galaxy Soccer Club. He was also seriously dreaming of them playing for the national soccer team. For this, Charles had mixed feelings because it could interfere with his graduate school aspirations; however he did not want to let Roberto down.

Chapter 5
Jill and Fred

Jill started working with Fred and acquiring the skills she needed for her experiment. Jill had to accomplish the placement of the catheters quickly because Fred would not wait very long for his 'screwdriver' before he started to throw a temper tantrum. She trained him to wait longer by holding and caressing one of his arms outside of the fence. She trained him to put his right hand and arm out through the fence to reach the drink while she offered another one to him through a small window that he had to reach with the left hand. She caressed and held his right arm while he was drinking and docile. She progressively accustomed him to enjoy the caressing and wait longer and longer for the drink.

She also observed the changes in Fred's facial demeanor when he was becoming impatient for his drink. Immediately before his rage attack, his pupils would dilate, precisely 10 seconds after the dilation he would show his large canine teeth and start hitting the fence with his left hand, pull his right arm from her and start jumping against the fence and biting the wire fiercely. His mouth would start bleeding from the contact of his gums with the wire. Fred would calm down only if she immediately placed the drink in his left hand window. He would take his drink and run away, annoyed. On the contrary, if she gave him the drink before the pupillary dilation, he would remain in the same spot and let her continue to caress his right arm through the fence.

She timed how long Fred would wait for his drink while she caressed his right arm before his pupils started to dilate. It was precisely seven minutes. That was the time she would have available to her to place the two catheters in his brachial artery and vein. As the pupils started to dilate she would inject the markers and 10 seconds later inject the anesthetic agent. Otherwise he would become wild; she would lose the catheters and possibly his hard gained confidence. She had to be efficient and precise. She had to go through a lot of training before she could finalize the experiment with the images of Fred's brain.

Two months before the date she had planned to perform the experiment, she volunteered to work in the blood collection room of the hospital's outpatient laboratory. There the IV technicians would canalize a vein with incredible efficiency. From 6 AM to 8 AM, more than one hundred fasting patients would have their blood collected by 6 technicians. She observed each one of them, how they held the needle, felt the vein under the skin and how they secured the needle, the catheter and how they canalized the vein. She became so acquainted with the technicians, always helping in a cheerful mood, that the supervisor offered her work there as a substitute when one of the technicians missed work. She eagerly took the opportunity. She became an expert on canalizing a vein and in the process actually made some money. She was able to canalize a vein, collect the blood and place a Band-Aid in the site of the puncture in less than two minutes. The technicians were in awe of her efficiency.

Every morning after her 2 hours at the blood collection laboratory, she went to spend time with Fred. Fred had become a friendly pet as long as he had his dose of vodka. He just had no interest in the life at the colony. He lived for his drink. At the same time, she enjoyed spending time with him, she was sorry for what he had become. Fred's lack of interest in his monkey life and his apparent depression was heartbreaking for Jill. Her sessions with Fred took one hour. Then she would go to the cardiac catheter laboratory where the cardiologists catheterized the arteries for heart arteriogram. Ten to fifteen patients with angina, a positive cardiac stress test and in danger of a heart attack had the exam every day.

Again, similar to her experience with the IV technicians, she observed the cardiologists' expertise. She was amazed with their ability to feel the artery's pulsation and place the catheter within few minutes. She had to do it herself to feel confident she could canalize Fred's artery in less than 5 minutes.

A student was not allowed to do this task in patients. Jill had to train her skills in the swine laboratory, where young interventional radiologists learned catheterization of arteries in order to perform placement of cardiac stents, arterioplasty, and other therapeutic maneuvers through arterial catheters. Jill eventually was able to catheterize the large swine femoral artery within 2 minutes. She then went to the animal surgical laboratory where brain-pacemakers were implanted in primates to control Parkinson's disease symptoms. She learned to catheterize their brachial arteries while they were anesthetized and became able to catheterize the monkey brachial artery within 2 minutes. She now felt confident that she could canalize the vein and the brachial artery of an anesthetized animal in four minutes. She actually had time to spare between the catheterization of Fred's blood vessels and the time his pupils started to dilate.

The question was: could she accomplish this with Fred awake, accessing his right arm outside of his cage through the chain-linked hole, while waiting for his drink? Would he react to the piercing of the needle? She had to get him used to piercing of his arm while she caressed him. He actually accepted the piercing of the needle amazingly well, letting her caress his arm and waiting for his drink. Fred was looking forward not only to the drink, but also to the time he spent with the loving creature that caressed his arm every day and fulfilled his needs for alcohol.

Jill was ready; she had the skills necessary to accomplish the planned experiment. She set the date for it and invited Charles to watch her and the laboratory team of scientists work. They all had learned to admire Jill's dedication and determination. She wanted proudly to show Charles what she had accomplished during those two summer months of intense work. Charles would help as a pair of extra hands if it became necessary. Since he had participated in developing Fred's cage, Jill felt that he was entitled to participate in this most important part of the effort—the actual experiment.

***

The laboratory group chose a Saturday because of the teaching and clinical commitments of the three professors directing the experiments. There was a pharmacologist, Dr. Mallory; a neurosurgeon, Dr. Hillary; and a chemist and behaviorist, Dr. Larsson. They had years of experience in animal research but had no time to acquire the invaluable skills that Jill was now mastering. They were proud of her accomplishments and confident that they would have a successful experiment. Dr. Larsson was especially amazed with Jill's capability to focus on a task and achieve such remarkable control of all aspects of the experimental protocol. This first experiment was an important step of several other steps that they would have to go through with Fred and Jill.

This was a feasibility experiment funded by the private donation from a grateful patient of Dr. Hillary to acquire pilot data in support of a proposal for large scale experiments funded by the National Institute of Health (NIH). The laboratory had estimated the series of experiments to cost 3 million dollars. The experiments were to last for three years. At the end of this period, Drs. Mallory and Hillary expected to have located a site in the brain to surgically implant a device to mitigate rage attacks. This implantable device was to be controlled by the patient as the patient wished. The ideal intervention should be minor surgery with no cognitive side-effects. The ambition of the project fitted perfectly inside Jill's dreams for a therapeutic measure for Charles.

Chapter 6
Jill and Fred and Charles and the Scientists

That Saturday morning, the team gathered at the laboratory at 7:00 AM. They had to prepare the drugs and the catheters before 9:00 AM, when Fred would be expecting his drink. Dr. Hillary brought Krispy-Kreme doughnuts and the group had a nice time around a fresh pot of coffee. Jill introduced Charles to Dr. Mallory, Dr. Larsson and Dr. Hillary.

Dr. Hillary congratulated Charles for his smart girlfriend. He remarked: "You will have a hard time keeping up with this intelligent woman."

"I do already," answered Charles promptly.

"You have a lot to learn about women, Charles. If she uses the skills she acquired working with Fred on you, she will wrap you around her fingers," said Dr. Hillary.

"I am looking forward to have the attention that she has given to Fred," continue Charles.

"Actually, you will have to accept some physical abuse from her before you guys get engaged. You know, she learned quite a bit about courtship observing the female monkeys. These ladies know how to select the best. I hope you will be able to tolerate the beating," insisted Dr. Hillary.

Although Charles understood the joke, because Jill had already explained to him the monkey's courtship behavior, he did not answer. He put his head down with this slightly insensitive joke. Deep inside he knew that tolerating any aggression was not something he could manage well. This lack of self-control depressed him, even though he knew that his sweet Jill would never abuse to him in any way. Dr. Hillary had no idea he had touched Charles so deeply.

Jill, however, understood Charles' awkwardness. She held his hand softly and tightened it. She immediately said, "Let's give some love to our Fred."

"Charles, don't be jealous. I am sure that you are smarter than Fred. At least you are not addicted to any drugs. I suggest you keep off them. Don't fry your brain; I cannot fix a fried brain," pressed Dr. Hillary with his out-of-place joke.

Charles recovered, "I should be jealous; he is getting most of Jill's attention. You need to finish this series of experiments soon, Jill."

"Yes, it will be nice when Fred is detoxified. It is depressing to see him so dependent on alcohol," said Jill.

"Yes, I also don't like to see his aggressive behavior," said Charles.

"Why?" Dr. Hillary asked.

"Let's talk about this later," intervened Jill, hoping to protect Charles from the possibly compromising answer. She didn't want to advertise Charles' disease to the laboratory people.

During that brief conversation over coffee and doughnuts, Dr. Hillary had probed Charles personality and interest in the science they were performing. He knew that Charles had developed all the activity sensors in Fred's cage and of his intentions of studying bioengineering from his conversations with Jill in the laboratory. As an experiment professor, Dr. Hillary was trying to gather all the information he needed to invite Charles to the other important part of this experimental undertaking, the development of the brain stimulation device. He didn't have enough time to discuss the issues fully with Charles, so he decided to invite the young couple for lunch after the experiment to continue the conversation.

***

"It is time to get started," uttered Dr. Mallory, as chief of the laboratory.

The group split up and each one went to their pressing task.

Charles and Dr. Mallory went to the room where Fred was kept. They had to bring him to the PET scan room. Dr. Hillary and Jill went to the PET room to prepare the catheters and the heparin-saline solution necessary to keep Fred's vein and artery from clotting and open for isotope and anesthetic injections. Despite his joking personality, Dr. Hillary was always providing friendly advice. He had a knack for getting into peoples' problems and helping naturally, as if he was an old friend. Dr. Hillary especially liked to work with young people, because of their naïve and prolific creativity. Dr. Hillary was already aware of Charles' sports and computer abilities from his conversations with Jill. He started to subtly explore Charles' personality; he was always trying to recruit intelligent young people to work in his scientific projects.

Dr. Larsson, a seasoned chemist specialized in radiopharmacology, went to the cyclotron to prepare the radioactive epinephrine and serotonin they were planning to inject just before Fred's pupillary dilation started. The experimental hypothesis was that the radioactive epinephrine would be captured by the cells that were primarily responsible for the initiation of the aggressive chain of reactions in the brain. The PET image would identify the site where the isotopes were captured. The radioactive serotonin would be sequestered in the areas of the brain where the cells were responsible for the onset of the depressive state that usually followed the rage attack.

They were all scheduled to be at the PET room at 8:45, and so they were. The cage was placed in a quiet corner of the room where Jill and Fred could stay alone. Jill had predicted that if Fred noticed too many people around him he would react differently than usual. Maybe his rage would start early, and she would not have the chance to place the catheters and inject the drugs as she was planning.

Dr. Larsson came on time from the cyclotron; this was a crucial step because of the short half-life of the isotopes. They had to be prepared immediately before the experiment to remain active at least until the PET detected them. Fred was acquainted also with Dr. Larson because he gave Fred his drink when Jill was in San Diego visiting Charles. Upon arrival, Dr. Larsson helped Jill with the catheterization. Jill had no difficulty placing the catheters, injecting the isotopes, and anesthetizing Fred at the exact moment when he was to develop the aggressive behavior. The PET was obtained without problems. The data had to be analyzed in the future with proper control scans for comparison, computer imaging subtraction and statistical analysis. This analysis was part of the future work that Jill would have to do; it was actually the most intellectually demanding part of her project.

Fred woke up after the experiment as if nothing had happened. He did not have the usual depression that followed his attacks. Dr. Larsson noted this peculiar fact and registered it in his observation log. Fred became active in his cage; Jill gave him his drink and the group congratulated each other for the successful experiment. Dr. Hillary reminded Jill that the next step was to obtain the electrical activity of Fred's brain during his rage attack. This promised to be a different challenge; however, more straightforward. This was because of the ingenious cage that Roberto and Charles had built.

Chapter 7
The Mentor

Dr. Hillary invited Charles and Jill for lunch to commemorate the successful experiment. Dr. Hillary loved to orient young people. He always had medical students, residents and post-graduate fellows following him around the hospital to learn his latest developed techniques and to take advantage of his vast experience taking care of patients and doing research. He was an Englishman that was always asking about the private affairs of the people that were around him. His philosophy was that the closer friend he could become of his students; the more he could help them. He knew of Jill's love for Charles and was most supportive of their future engagement. He wanted to be sure, however, that their personal involvement would not jeopardize Jill's and Charles promising future. He wanted to help them to sort out study, work and sports in a balanced and pleasant fashion.

Dr. Hillary had played soccer in his youth; he was a fan of European soccer. Dr. Hillary encouraged Charles to pursue both bioengineering and professional soccer. He presented to Charles his plan to develop a microelectrode connected to a smart electronic system with the ability to record and electrically modulate specific areas of the brain when it became necessary to block undesirable symptoms in different diseases. Dr. Hillary's scientific ideas excited Charles. He understood that if Dr. Hillary's scientific dreams came true it could be the solution for his own rage and depression attacks. Charles committed himself to helping Dr. Hillary with his attempts to perfect a smart modulating device for the central nervous system.

Dr. Hillary explained to Charles that this was a long-term project that was already begun in one of the bioengineering laboratories of the university. They still needed a young and dedicated scientist to perform the interface of the device with the living animal. Charles and Jill could work well together in this endeavor. The timing was correct; while Jill prepared herself to be a surgeon, Charles would prepare himself as a bioengineer. They had more than 5 years of study ahead of them before they could accomplish the tasks needed to make a device ready for human implant.

"What do you think about the idea of modulating the brain electronically, Charles?" Dr. Hillary asked.

"Fantastic and cool," answered Charles. "Is it realistic?"

"Every scientific dream is realistic if the scientist works on it consistently, intelligently and with passion," remarked Dr. Hillary.

"Great! I am on!" Charles knew he had the passion; it was his livelihood.

"I believe that you and Jill make the perfect team to bring this dream to fruition. Today, Jill has shown consistency, talent dealing with animals, and intelligence. You have impressed me with your computerized cage. That was quite a mechanic electronic computer integration. You showed, as did Jill, consistency, talent, and intelligence. The only question I have is if you both have enough passion."

Jill and Charles gazed at each other. That eye contact carried all their hope for a future of a happy and loving life. They knew they had more than enough passion. They felt awkward to enter in such a personal matter with Dr. Hillary. It was still too early to open up to him. Jill feared that Dr. Hillary would not give Charles an opportunity if he knew that Charles had such a difficult emotional problem. They changed the subject.

"Dr. Hillary, I heard that you were an excellent soccer player in England, I love soccer," said Charles.

"Yes, those were good times. I loved playing. Medical school took me away from soccer though. I became passionate about science. I guess it was worthwhile, I love what I do," said Dr. Hillary.

"I am sure that was hard for you to make a decision between soccer and science," said Jill, exploring some guidance for Charles.

"It was not. I just let it happened naturally. I kept on playing soccer and dedicating my extra time to science, until the day I noticed that I was playing scientist and dedicating my extra time to soccer. I became older, my brain got better, and my legs got worse. Naturally I had to stay with science. That is how I usually make my decisions; I let them happen naturally. I just keep doing my best in all fields I am involved; it always works for the best. Let your passion guide your life; don't drop your talents."

"There is time for everything you want to accomplish. There is no reason why you cannot play professional soccer and still finish college and start graduate school. The busier you become, the less in trouble you will get into. If you love soccer as you say Charles, I suggest that you give it the best you have. Don't let an opportunity pass by. Your true call, either sports or academics will show itself in due time," Dr. Hillary finished.

At this point, Jill felt comfortable and expressed her concern about Charles' volatility and a professional soccer career. Dr. Hillary felt that the challenge would be a great exercise for his mental control. He also suggested that Charles should seek to diversify his friendship in the college soccer team. This would introduce more colleagues ready to help him if he needed to be stopped. Charles mentioned his gratitude and dedication to Roberto's friendship and how he was worried of letting him down regarding the professional soccer opportunities. Dr. Hillary reassured him that he was not responsible for Roberto's success. Roberto should hold on his own first. It was commendable that he was so loyal to this friend, but if Charles increased the close circle of friends around his and Roberto's soccer, this would only increase their opportunities and his security at the soccer field. Charles quickly understood the concept and smiled to Dr. Hillary in approval of his ideas.

From this moment on, Dr. Hillary became an integral part of Charles' and Jill's lives. They confided to him all their problems. Dr. Hillary was extremely busy with grant writing, patient care, teaching and traveling to conventions, but always took the time to listen to them and advise them to the best of his knowledge. Dr. Hillary started also to create traveling opportunities for Jill to present her initial findings in the laboratory. Jill went to scientific meetings to report her experiences with the behavior of the monkeys in the colony. This scientific background she was acquiring would be invaluable to help her enter into medical school.

Dr. Hillary was preparing her for the steep competition she would encounter while applying. The acceptance was based on grades, community work, scientific experience, and extracurricular activities. The same criteria were applied for Charles to gain entrance into the bioengineering school; however, the competition was much less fierce. Charles would have time to play professional soccer for a while.

After lunch, Charles and Jill said goodbye to Dr. Hillary, expressed their gratitude for the opportunities he was creating for them and went to enjoy the rest of the weekend. They decided to roller blade in the strand of Santa Monica beach. They arrived there at 4 PM. The breeze from the ocean was mild and the sun was starting to approach the horizon. They headed south in the strand; the exercise became more and more intense. Jill was a dedicated ice skater until age thirteen. This gave her incredible skills and speed with the roller blade. Charles could barely keep up with her.

After one hour of intense skating, they fell in the sand to observe the sun set. Jill's face was sweaty, her eyes bright and large and her respiration was rapid, bringing her breasts up and down in an exciting fashion for Charles. As he concentrated on the waving of her chest and the ocean waves, his love for her invaded his chest. He embraced her feeling the pressure in his chest that he felt the night they first made love in Jill's studio. They rolled in the sand and kissed deeply. Pulling back from her, Charles smiled, and wiped sand off Jill's cheek.

"You are so special, Jill… Will you marry me?" he asked.

He sat up and pulled a small box out of his pocket. Jill opened it, and her eyes widened when she saw the delicate diamond ring he had saved for this moment.

"What a complete day… Are you sure about what you said, Charlie? I would like to hear it again," whispered Jill.

"I love you and want to spend my whole life with you, would you marry me?" whispered Charles, gazing deeply her large, wet, and dark brown eyes.

"Charlie, it's what I want the most, we're great together."

"I feel the same. I'm so proud of you. Your skills with Fred were so impressive. I admire you so much. I have no doubt that I want to dedicate my life to our lives," said Charles.

"I feel that we will be so happy together. Dr. Hillary opened up my eyes further for the wonderful future we can have together. I feel that we have the tools to fight your rage problem. We just need to dedicate this initial part of our lives to build a wonderful future for us and our future children," said Jill.

"When he expressed doubt if we had enough passion to conduct the research project, I almost screamed, you bet we do, Dr. Hillary!" Charles laughed.

"What an opportunity, Charlie. I'm so excited with such a useful project. I feel so privileged to have the opportunity to work on our problem. I feel I am dreaming. I want this day to last forever," said Jill.

"Let's go home and celebrate," said Charles.

"The ring is so beautiful. Thank you! Thank you! I love you!" She held his hand while they skated back home.

Chapter 8
Soccer

Despite his parents' concerns, Charles was quick to answer yes when Roberto announced that his father had heard from the Galaxy coach that they should try for the team. They were to receive the invitation letter early that fall. Roberto and Charles decided not to discuss the subject with his parents until they had the letters in hand. Charles and Roberto had long conversations with Mr. Hernandez in order to strategically try to maintain their position together in the new team. Their partnership was important for the success of both. The challenge was to show the Galaxy's coach, Mr. Pirelli, that together they were better than the arrangement that Mr. Pirelli already had in his team.

Mr. Claude Pirelli was a constantly screaming coach and very hardheaded. He was not very happy with how his team did the previous season. He was planning to inject new blood in the team while maintaining his well-known stellar players. For the positions that Charles and Roberto had in the college team, Mr. Pirelli already had two outstanding players, the mid-fielder Chris Brass, and the forward Brandy Muller. Charles and Roberto had to excel individually and as a duo to take these players' places.

Charles received the letter on a Thursday afternoon. Excitedly, he showed it to his mother.

"Charles, have you thought this professional soccer issue through? Will this disturb your grad school?"

"Mom, I want to play. I'll do both, grad school and soccer. I know I can do well in both. It is a great opportunity. I also need the salary to prepare for my marriage," said Charles with conviction.

"I am not sure this is a good idea. We have to reason this with your father. You know that he would rather see you put all your efforts into your academic career," said his Mrs. Morales.

"Mom, I have thought this through. Although I can get into fights in the field, professional soccer is played in a very secure environment. Even if I become violent, I will always be surrounded by people that will stop me short of seriously hurting someone," said Charles.

"I guess so," agreed his mother anxiously.

"I talked to one of Jill's professors at UCLA, Dr. Hillary; he played professional soccer. He said that soccer is the best way for me to practice controlling my temper. I'll work hard on it. I need to get over this handicap," he uttered sadly.

"Well, talk to your dad over dinner. Let's hear what he says," said his mother with a loving smile.

That afternoon, Charles called Jill to gather her support. He was surprised with her enthusiastic response.

"Go, Charlie, you will do great! We need the money, it will help us to be together more often," said Jill.

"Thanks, I love you!"

Charles felt secure in his decision. At dinnertime, he announced to his father the news. Mr. Morales' reaction was of extreme caution.

"Charles, we discussed this before. You need a protected environment and to avoid direct confrontation. A grad school laboratory where you can be creative is the best place for you. You are outstanding in exact sciences. Your computer skills will help you excel. Please reconsider your decision," Mr. Morales said calmly.

"Dad, I want to be a bioengineer, mostly I want to work with Jill and Dr. Hillary on their project. However, there is no reason for me not to play soccer also."

"Charles, professional soccer is too demanding. Traveling, hours of practice and concentration will take you away from your studies. You know that lack of sleep, poor nutrition and irregular hours aggravate your condition," remarked Mr. Morales.

"Dad, I promise I will be careful," replied Charles.

"You know best, you obviously have thought this through. I want to be proved wrong. I will certainly enjoy watching you playing soccer on TV; actually, some fighting always makes watching games on TV more exciting." He smiled.

Charles and Roberto signed their contracts and started practicing soccer with the Galaxy in the second week of September. Their schedule became crazy. They had no time to visit Jill. School full-time and soccer full-time was all they could do. School started suffering for both. Their grades deteriorated. Mr. Morales was always talking to Charles about his priorities, but Charles was challenged by the competition of making the team. He was sitting on the bench most of the games. Roberto had started to play half games as a midfielder; however, the high scoring of his college games was not happening. Brandy Muller, the established Galaxy high scorer striker, was not converting Roberto's passes into goals. Roberto was also not having the free kick opportunities that Charles provided him in the college games.

Coach Pirelli was becoming unhappy with Roberto's performance. The team was losing most of the games and Coach Pirelli would not try Roberto and Charles together. Charles always entered as a left-winger, away from Roberto's position and without any support for his fast scoring. The reality was that Brandy Muller was a major star; Mr. Pirelli was always giving him the opportunity until the last minute, hoping that he would score, but he was not carrying the team to victories.

Mr. Hernandez approached Coach Pirelli angrily, asking him to play Roberto and Charles together. But this made matters only worse. Pirelli was too hardheaded to listen. Roberto and Charles were getting discouraged; they were not being able to excel in soccer or in school. Charles was also not having time to see Jill; he would spend more than two months without seeing her during the soccer season. He was ready to break down and quit soccer. One weekend he managed to drive to Los Angeles with Roberto to see Jill. She had arranged a Sunday brunch with Dr. Hillary. She was relying more and more on his friendship and guidance.

Dr. Hillary, Jill, Roberto, and Charles went out for lunch in the Westwood Village. Jill had already prepared Dr. Hillary for Charles' depression over the last few months. Charles was indeed discouraged; he was losing interest not only in soccer, but also in school. Charles' long periods of depression worried Jill for he would even stop calling her. She could not help but drawing a parallel between Charles and Fred's behavior. She was hoping that Dr. Hillary could reach out to Charles and advise him.

At lunch, Dr. Hillary started: "So, Charles, how is life?"

"Not as I had planned," answered Charles, gazing down.

"What about yours, Roberto?" Dr. Hillary asked.

"It is getting better. I am starting to have some playing time. School has been tough though," remarked Roberto.

"Well, you two have to shape up, school has to be outstanding, and soccer has to be outstanding. Figure out a way to improve! Charlie, thinking that life is tough will not make you successful. I want to see more effort from both of you. Work more and sleep less! Your girlfriend here is excelling in the laboratory and at school; what kind of men are you?" Dr. Hillary started laughing.

"If I don't sleep well, I become very aggressive," said Charles.

"Maybe you need a little more aggressiveness to impress Coach Pirelli." Dr. Hillary replied.

Jill worried about this comment. She did not know if Charles could monitor his own aggressiveness and stop when appropriate. She intervened, changing the subject, "We are taking a difficult statistics course this semester. Charlie, you may be able to help me with it. Let's study together during your free weekends. You can help Roberto and me. We will make it," said Jill.

They continued the conversation. Dr. Hillary was very clear to Roberto and Charles that they had to push to the limits. He suggested that they challenge Coach Pirelli, promising a victory if he gave them a chance. Jill set up a schedule for them to be together during the weekends and spend most of the time studying. She was planning to drive to San Diego to save Roberto and Charles time. They finished lunch with plans that made Charles less depressed. He always looked forward to spending time with Jill. He was also willing to challenge Coach Pirelli, since he had nothing to lose.

***

There was a game scheduled for the following weekend. Charles and Roberto talked to their coach about their frustration and their hope for an opportunity to play together.

Claude Pirelli did not budge; he simply answered, "I make the decisions regarding the team."

However, he was starting to seriously consider Charles and Roberto's requests. He liked Charles and Roberto because of their exemplary behavior and their respect toward him and to their teammates. They were unselfish players. They had great skills; they were humble and great colleagues. Their teammates were also starting to suggest to Coach Pirelli that they would like to see Charles having more playing time. They were disappointed with Brandy Muller's performance and his slight arrogance. Even his best friend in the team, Chris Brass, the mid-fielder supporting him, was getting disappointed. Brandy made little effort during the games; he mostly waited for the proper opportunity to score. If his teammates did not provide him with the perfect ball, he would accomplish nothing and complain bitterly. After a game that they lost, Brandy complained about Roberto to Mr. Pirelli.

"Coach, Roberto is too slow forwarding the ball from the midfield. By the time the ball gets to me, two defenders are already on me. It is impossible to play with him."

Charles, who was spending most of the time on the bench observing the game, could not take it. He immediately said, "You are the one not trying. I sure would love to have the passes you received from Roberto today. You were not doing much either when Chris Brass was in the midfield during the first half. He also served you some very good ones."

Charles was pressing Coach Pirelli for an opportunity as Dr. Hillary had suggested. He just did not realize how strongly Brandy would react to his direct criticism.

"Charles, I do the talking, make the judgments and take the decisions, you just listen!" yelled Mr. Pirelli and continued, "Brandy you have not done well for ages. You are not only making no effort; you are also not using your brain. You are playing a lazy game."

"That's not fair! I'll talk with you later, Charlie," Brandy screamed, threatening Charles.

Coach Pirelli disregarded this remark and went on, "I already told you all many times, the ball does not have a brain, you have to use your own and guide the ball properly. This requires physical and intellectual effort. Mostly you have to play together. You have to be aware of the position of each of your teammates in the whole soccer field. That is why each of you has to keep your position; it facilitates your teammate finding you when he needs you. Make yourselves available. When the ball comes to you, control it, look for your teammates and think! Serve them with a perfect pass. Don't waste time and energy kicking ball around without purpose."

He looked to Charlie and Brandy and changed his tone:

"Charlie and Brandy, I don't want to see fighting among teammates. I will suspend both of you if I hear that you are mouthing off at each other. Next game you start playing together, I want to see passing and courtesy on the field. Let's see if you can use your brains constructively."

He continued, "We are almost the last team in the league this year. We will have to practice more and become a tighter group. I want to enhance our opportunity to score; that is why we will need Charlie and Brandy together in the next game. I want to see our offense playing like a charm! Our defense is doing its job; we are not losing by large scores. We are just not scoring. Now you go rest, I will see you Monday afternoon."

Charlie was tired and hungry; disappointed with the lack of opportunity Mr. Pirelli was giving him and upset by Brandy's threatening remark. He immediately grabbed his soccer bag and bolted to the parking lot ahead of Roberto. Roberto stayed, talking with Coach Pirelli about his performance. Roberto was concerned that the coach would listen to Brandy's accusations. Charlie put his bag in the back of Roberto's pickup truck and waited. He was looking down, distracted, supporting his elbows over the edge of the pickup truck bed and thinking about the game when he was pushed from behind.

"Here guy, the next time you say anything about my game, I'll make you swallow your tongue," said Brandy, pointing his finger at Charles' face.

Chris Brass was with Brandy. They were longtime friends. Chris said, "Let's go, Brandy, he is not worth our time, he doesn't even make the team! You saw, he didn't play more than 10 minutes today."

"No, this chicken-shit has to learn not to mess with me," replied Brandy.

Charles turned to walk away without saying anything, but Brandy pushed him again. Charles looked down and unexpectedly punched Brandy's stomach. Brandy bent down with pain and Charles punched him again in the mouth. Blood started running from his mouth, gushing through the nose. Brandy started coughing, but Charles was charged with rage. When he saw the blood, his aggressive instincts intensified. He punched Brandy again in the stomach with the right hand and followed with a left in his forehead. Brandy immediately fell unconscious.

Chris stayed paralyzed and horrified with Charles' violence. Charles looked at Chris with an enraged face and moved fast in his direction. Chris backed up but Charles was already over him. Charles grabbed Chris' neck, locking it under his arm. Chris asked for mercy, but Charles was already tightening his neck to a point that Chris was not being able to speak. Suddenly Roberto walked out of the building and saw Brandy in the ground and Chris gasping for air under Charles' arm. He screamed, "Charlie, what are you doing? Let him go now!"

Charles looked up and saw his friend's face; he recognized his expression of horror. Charles woke up from his aggressive trance, let Chris go and looked around. When he saw the blood over Brandy's body, he fell on the ground, covered his face with his hands and started sobbing aloud. At this moment, Couch Pirelli walked into the parking lot and saw the scene. He immediately called 911 on his cell phone and rushed to help Brandy. Brandy did not wake up, however. Chris remained on the ground gasping for air and rubbing his neck. Roberto grabbed Charles and walked him to his pickup truck. He closed the door and went to help Mr. Pirelli to attempt to revive Brandy.

The paramedics arrived a few minutes later. They also could not revive Brandy. He was breathing, however. They cleared his airway with suction and inserted a tracheal tube to assure proper respiration. They stabilized his neck carefully; at this point the bleeding had stopped and the blood pressure was normal. Brandy's pupils were small and reacted to light. The paramedics rushed him to the hospital emergency.

Roberto took Charles home. Charles would not stop crying. When Mrs. Morales saw his condition, she immediately took him to the psychiatric emergency room. He was admitted and placed on heavy sedation.

Coach Pirelli drove Chris home. Chris was also in shock but had recovered enough to tell Mr. Pirelli the story. Chris was honest, he told Mr. Pirelli that Brandy pushed Charles twice, and that he threatened him. He also told that Charles tried to avoid the fight and that Brandy continued to push him. Then he told of the incredible violence that suddenly overtook Charles. He described his face as that of an enraged animal.

"Charles was out of his mind," he said.

He also described the way Charles stared at him when Charles overtook him. Chris was not angry with Charles; he understood that Charles was not himself when he attacked him. Chris also felt guilty of his demeaning remark that probably triggered Charles' attack. Chris was still scared and wanting to go home. Mr. Pirelli dropped him off at his house after advising Chris' mother that he would be excused from playing for the next month.

When Brandy arrived in the emergency room, he was already awake and fighting to remove the tube from his throat. His pupils were reactive and of normal size. He would follow simple commands, such as showing correct numbers when asked to show one or two fingers. This was an excellent sign. However, the doctor in the emergency room sedated him and asked for a tomography of his brain. He had to rule out the possibility of intracranial bleeding. This was important because if there were active intracranial bleeding Brandy would soon lose conscious again and progress to severe coma and possibly death, if the bleeding was not controlled by surgery. The tomography was performed; there was no intracranial hemorrhage or bruises in the brain.

Brandy was transferred to the intensive care unit and allowed to wake up. The endotracheal tube was removed, and he was discharged to the regular ward that same evening. The next day he was completely normal and was discharged home with the diagnosis of a mild concussion. He had merely experienced a complete electrical discharge of his brain with the blow that Charles gave to his forehead. It took a little longer for his brain to recharge because he also hit the back of his head in the pavement of the parking lot. He had only few cuts inside of his mouth. Fortunately for him and Charles, he recovered well. However, Brandy was completely enraged and pressed charges against Charles for physical assault.

Charles remained one week in the psychiatric hospital. He was allowed out of heavy sedation the next morning after the fight. However, he continued very depressed. He did not want to eat or talk. The doctor started him on antidepressants and kept him under observation. ECT was suggested, however Charles' mother did not allow. Although Charles had not expressed suicidal thoughts, it was not uncommon for young men to kill themselves when they were in such a state of depression. Charles started to interact with the nurses and the doctor three days later and asked to go home by the end of the week.

Knowing that Charles' mother was a psychiatric nurse, the doctor let him go home the next weekend. Charles stayed out of soccer for the following six weeks. He spent every weekend studying with Jill and Roberto. Their presence cheered him up fast. Three weeks after the fight, he was already asking his mother to stop the medication and to return to soccer.

Six weeks after the fight, Charles returned to practice. He was received warmly by his teammates. Charles was mostly surprised with Chris Brass' behavior. He came to talk with him and apologized:

"Sorry Charles, I was wrong that afternoon. I hope you feel well. We missed you in practice."

Charles was ashamed of his attack on Chris. He knew he had overreacted. He answered: "I'm sorry also; I should have let it go. We would not have missed all this game time. Mostly, Brandy and I wouldn't have ended up in the hospital."

"Charlie, forget it, it's all over. Let's have a great season; we need to recover our team ranking. Without our help Galaxy lost the last two games," said Chris.

"It's not quite over, Brandy pressed charges against me. I'll have to answer to that," said Charles.

"No, Charlie. I went to the police and told them the true story. I told them that you acted in self-defense. When I said that Brandy touched you first, they will drop the charges if your lawyer makes a good case. Don't you worry anymore, I'll serve as witness," said Chris cordially.

Charles felt at ease and asked, "What about Brandy?"

"Well, he's pissed off with me, but he will come around. He practiced last week. He will come to practice today. He's not talking to me," said Chris.

"I'm sorry. You were good friends."

"Yes, we've played together now for more than three years. Brandy has changed though. His success went up to his head. Lately it has been difficult to relate to him. He is more interested on lots of girls and partying. I like that too, but within limits," said Chris, smiling.

"Do you think he is getting tired of soccer?" asked Charles.

"No, he is only twenty-four. He has a long career ahead of him. If he decides to clean himself up and work hard, he is a great candidate for the national team. He almost made it to the last World Cup three years ago."

Roberto, who was observing at distance, approached them when he saw both smiling.

"Coach Pirelli is calling us. He wants to see how you are doing, Charles. If you play well today, he will start you next Saturday in the beginning of the game," said Roberto cheerfully.

While they walked, Chris asked, "Charlie, are you in shape? Six weeks without playing is a lot."

"Yes. Actually, the reason I recovered so fast is because Roberto made me run four hours every day since I left the hospital. I feel great!"

The practice went well. Roberto, Chris, and Charlie played well together. Chris and Roberto were dominating the midfield, giving great opportunities to Charles and Brandy, who had arrived late. Charles also served great balls to Brandy. Brandy did not direct a single word to Charles. He avoided passing the ball to Charles and he actually intercepted passes going to Charles several times. Charles scored more goals in the scrimmage than any other player. Coach Pirelli was convinced that Charles was ready to start playing on Saturday. He was still hopeful that Charles and Brandy could develop a relationship on the field that would bring victories to the team. He wanted to try his strategy of a very offense-oriented team. Both Charles and Brandy were very aggressive players.

Mr. Pirelli started Charles playing side by side with Brandy. He expected Charles to provide the perfect opportunities for Brandy and advised Charles to do so. Roberto stayed on the bench. In the middle of the first half, Charlie received a pass from Chris and looked for Brandy who should had forced into the box, but Brandy had not followed through to receive the ball. Charles had to dribble the last defender, enter the box alone and come face to face with the goalkeeper. Before he could try to score, the sweeper that he had just dribbled past kicked his legs from behind. He fell and angrily jumped up to hit the defender; luckily, the goalkeeper grabbed Charles' legs. He fell again. Brandy was close by and pushed the sweeper from behind over Charles.

The referee gave a yellow card to Brandy, to the sweeper and to the goalkeeper. He assigned a penalty kick to the Galaxy. Brandy kicked and missed the goal. Coach Pirelli became livid with Brandy. He not only had instigated a fight against Charles, but also had lost a great opportunity for the Galaxy. He took him out of the game, putting Roberto in his place.

Mr. Pirelli instructed Roberto to play just behind Charles and control the midfield with Chris' help. Charles became the striker. They had only 5 minutes in the first half to play. Roberto and Charles managed to score a goal, again by Charles receiving a penalty inside of the box. Roberto kicked a perfect penalty kick. The second half of the game was even more exciting; they managed to score another three goals. Charles scored two and Chris one. The score ended 4 x 2. Coach Pirelli was convinced that Chris, Charles, and Roberto should play together.

Charles and Roberto played entire game from then on. Charles was expelled once for punching a goalkeeper in one of the games. Brandy sat on the bench for the rest of the season and his contract with the Galaxy was not renewed. Chris, Roberto, and Charles became the core of the Galaxy offense. For the rest of the season, the Galaxy lost only in the semifinal, the same game in which Charles hit the goalkeeper and was expelled from the game.

Chapter 9
Desperation

Jill was desperate. She remained in San Diego for a whole week in the aftermath of Charles' fight with Brandy. She became frightened with what had happened. She was seeing that Charles could not be left alone without a serious risk of getting into major trouble. Upon returning to Los Angeles, she went to speak with Dr. Hillary, hoping for some therapeutic suggestion. Mostly she was hopeful for surgery. By now, she had read about several surgical procedures for aggressive behavior. She was becoming convinced that Charles needed surgery. He definitively was not able to control himself when rage set in.

Operations were used in the past but were outlawed in several states of the nation. Where psychosurgery was allowed the criteria for approval of one of these surgeries became very stringent. She hoped, however, that with the help of Dr. Hillary, Charles could be a candidate for a procedure that would tide him over; at least until their laboratory work was more advanced. Charles needed help now; she was seeing him getting more and more in trouble with the police. He was lucky that the lawyer was able to clear him from the last two incidents. However, these incidents would certainly affect his future as a professional.

"Dr. Hillary, Charles got into a major fight last weekend, I am so scared, we need to do something soon," said Jill.

"Why are you so anxious, was it really a serious fight?" asked Dr. Hillary.

"He knocked one of his teammates unconscious and almost strangled another one. One of them pressed charges; again, he had to deal with the police. He's still in the hospital, where he will stay for three weeks. I'm afraid that he will kill someone one of these days," said Jill.

"Jill, a surgery for behavior modification is not to be taken lightly. Especially in California, the law is very strict," Dr. Hillary answered.

"I am sure that you can go around the law to help Charlie, otherwise he will get in trouble with the law," Jill anxiously said.

"It is not possible to go around the law, Jill. If any complication happens, I can lose my license to practice and even end up in jail!" replied Dr. Hillary emotionally.

"I am seeing Charlie going to jail for years one of these days if we don't do something. Worse is that he knows it too. He was deeply depressed when I left him in the hospital. His psychiatrist said that he is suicidal, they wanted even to give him ECT," Jill said, sobbing.

"I have been working during the past 10 years to assemble a team of physicians that would participate in psychosurgery; however the issue is too politically charged. Doctors don't want to run the risk of a bad press," said Dr. Hillary.

"Why do you need a team of physicians, why can't you make the decision yourself? You know Charles has a serious problem. You know he is willing to undergo surgery if surgery controls his aggressive attacks," Jill said.

"The state of California requires a committee of doctors to approve a psychosurgery. It is required that the treating psychiatrist and the surgeon performing the surgery sign a declaration that this is a measure of last resort, almost a compassionate treatment," Dr. Hillary said.

"This can be arranged," insisted Jill.

"There are more requirements, but this simple one is already very difficult. Even if I am the surgeon on record and sign the declaration, we don't have a psychiatrist who would be willing to sign it. Charles has not followed a complete psychiatric drug trial for a period of several years. I don't believe that he will be willing to go through it at this time in his life," Dr. Hillary said.

"Why not?" Jill asked.

"Jill, you know the side-effects of the drugs that he has taken in the past. Taking those drugs would prevent him from playing soccer. Moreover, they would disturb his studies. Charles was very emphatic that he doesn't want to take drugs. I partially agree with him," concluded Dr. Hillary.

"We need to reconsider this issue with him, Dr. Hillary. It is better to take drugs than end up in jail," Jill said.

"Let's continue. Even if a psychiatrist supports Charles' surgery, we will still need to fulfill the other requirements of the state law. We will need a physician appointed by the hospital and more; a psychiatrist and a neurosurgeon appointed by the county of Los Angeles, also to approve of the surgery. This will not be easy," said Dr. Hillary.

"It is not impossible," said Jill, starting to get frustrated with Dr. Hillary's negativism.

"Obviously, Charles' parents have to agree with this and sign an informed consent; Charles has to sign it also. Minors are not allowed to undergo psychosurgery in this state. Is Charles more than 18?" Dr. Hillary asked.

"Yes, he is 20 now, almost 21," Jill said impatiently.

"Great, this is the only easy part. The major difficulty is that I don't have a good surgery for Charlie," Dr. Hillary said, sighing.

"Dr. Hillary, I don't believe you. What about lesions in special areas of the brain such as amygdalotomy or hypothalamotomy?" Jill challenged.

"These destructive surgeries were used in the past. Destruction of the amygdale or hypothalamus, areas of the brain believed to control behavior were done the past, usually for the mental retarded and criminals. The side-effects are less than desirable, actually formidable. Charles may lose the ability to have emotions. Imagine, he no longer would love or care for you," said Dr. Hillary.

Jill had so much hoped that Dr. Hillary would find a way to help her. She couldn't believe that he would accept such a limitation.

"Jill, doctors have committed too many mistakes in the past, that is why there are so many laws limiting our work. Lawyers make an incredible living by stepping in between patients and their doctors. Legal issues have skyrocketed the prices of medical care. Insurance companies don't miss the opportunity to portray doctors as dishonest and careless people so they can collect huge malpractice insurance policy money."

"So what? We need to help Charlie! Money shouldn't be an issue. We are talking about his quality of life and the safety of other people's lives," Jill said.

"Jill, you need to learn more about the history of psychosurgery to understand my hesitation," replied Dr. Hillary and started telling Jill the history.

"It all started thousands of years ago when trepanations were performed to release bad spirits. It is registered in history that in 2000 BC the Egyptians were practicing trepanation in the Pharaohs skull just before their death, in the hope that they would be saved. The Incas in Peru, 1000 AD, also practiced trepanation, with some of the patients surviving. However, it was a Portuguese, Egas Moniz, who first introduced psychosurgery to our currently practiced medicine. He actually earned the Nobel Prize of Medicine in 1949 for his descriptions of the bilateral frontal lobotomy. This operation became popular all over the world. Doctors seeking fame and money did it indiscriminately.

Side-effects and complications were under reported. When one reads the reports of those times, it seems that psychosurgery could cure all," Dr. Hillary said.

"I have read some of them. I read the work of Dr. Ballantine in Boston. He was very careful," Jill said.

"He was already part of the new generation when stereotactic surgery was widely used. Neurosurgery reached mathematical precision with this technique," Dr. Hillary answered.

"Psychosurgery was more prominent here in this country when the psychiatric hospitals were overcrowded with the veterans of the World War II. It is estimated that between 1936 and 1978 some 35000 operations were performed in the USA. It was Freeman who developed the 'icepick' technique that became infamous with the movie of Fannie Farmer's life. He lost the collaboration of his neurosurgeon colleague Dr. Watts, who disagreed with his indiscriminate practice of psychosurgery, and his lack of respect to the most common rules of surgical sterility."

"Since he didn't have the most basic training of surgery, he had to develop the 'icepick' approach. He put the patients to sleep with a session of ECT. While they were unconscious, he broke the roof of their orbit with the icepick and severed their frontal lobe connections with a blind sweep of a needle. Countless patients died of infection and/or intracranial bleeding. These terrible events were kept from the public knowledge by the walls of the psychiatric institutions where he performed his surgery."

"Dr. Freeman, then a famous psychiatrist, made some abusive remarks. He said that he could perform 50 of such operations in the course of a single day. He stated that he had found the solution for the overcrowded mental hospitals that were in shortage of everything, except of patients. He remarked that psychosurgery was more effective in blacks and women. These racist and prejudicial comments, coupled with the surgery's side-effects, leaked out from the walls of the psychiatric institutions, were documented and had profound social implications."

"Famous people were permanently altered by psychosurgery. The novel of Ken Kesey, *One Flew Over the Cuckoo's Nest*, in 1958, later turned into a five Oscar winning movie in 1978 was the final blow. The public opinion in Los Angeles built up to street riots, enforcing restrictive laws to psychosurgery. Psychosurgery was depicted to the public as a potential way of controlling people, including politically. Because of the misbehaviors of our fellow physicians, the science of psychosurgery is now years behind and unable to help patients in real need, like your Charlie," Dr. Hillary concluded.

"Dr. Hillary, this is the past. Charles is living now, we need to help him!" Jill said.

"Yes Jill, that is why I assembled the team to develop a surgical treatment for psychiatric diseases. I believe that with the technology available we can perfect a surgery devoid of the side-effects that so much destroyed the acceptance of psychosurgery. I believe that when we have an effective surgical treatment, with acceptable side-effects and reversible at the patient's will, it will be easy to overcome the laws and social issues," Dr. Hillary remarked.

"But what do we do now about Charlie?" asked Jill desperately.

"Let's bring him close to us and protect him. Let's provide him with an environment in which he may thrive as a scientist. Let's study him. Let's make him understand all aspects of his own disease so he can help us make proper decisions. You and I can do it. I count so much on you and Charles for help with this project. You have the passion we need to complete this effort," Dr. Hillary said, holding Jill's hand and smiling at her.

Her eyes were large and wet; she didn't know what to say. She let Dr. Hillary squeeze her hand and sobbed. That night, Jill decided that she wanted to bring Charles to Los Angeles as soon as possible. Maybe he should stop playing soccer, transfer to UCLA and finish his last year of college, she thought. She saw the possibility of marrying him next spring and bringing him to Los Angeles in the fall. She discussed her thoughts with Dr. Hillary.

He assured her he would help Charles enter the bioengineering graduate program at UCLA. He should apply for it.

Chapter 10
Jealousy

Jill and Charles decided that they would marry that spring. Charles' success in soccer had been astonishing. Together with Roberto and Chris he was invited to play for the national team. The World Cup was scheduled to be in Los Angeles that summer. He was preparing for the games and at the same time had a full school schedule. He was comfortable financially; although soccer did not pay much in the USA, he was able to afford a small flat in Westwood. Because of his constant trips all over the country and sometimes internationally, Charles was spending most of the time away from his parents' home in San Diego. Roberto and Chris became his constant companions. He was never left alone.

When in Los Angeles, he would stay with Jill in their flat. Roberto and Chris also rented a flat in Westwood; this facilitated their driving together with Charles to soccer practice in Gardena. Despite his erratic schedule, Charles was able to cope with school and soccer. Roberto took the year off from school to concentrate on the World Cup. Chris had already finished college and was only playing soccer.

Spring was upon them. The training for the World Cup intensified. The Galaxy offered its new home stadium in Gardena to be the home of the USA national team. Charlie, now already enrolled for the last year of college at UCLA, was spending more time with Jill. The drive from UCLA to the stadium was short enough that Charlie was now living with Jill in their flat in Westwood. Their marriage was scheduled for the end of May. Jill was excited with the preparations. She had also progressed with her experiments with Fred.

Jill had finished all the studies on aggressive behavior with Fred and was now working on obtaining the normal function of Fred's brain during an attack of rage, while not under alcohol addiction. She worked for several months with him to stop his alcohol addiction. She continued with the same routine of giving him his 'screwdriver' every day and caressing his arm through the chain link fence. She progressively diluted the amount of vodka. After two months, Fred was happy drinking only orange juice. He was not having his rage fits for alcohol. Most interesting is that Fred looked forward to his orange juice and the caressing of his arm. Jill had provided that gentle touch over the two years of experimentation. Fred was now participating actively in his monkey's life in the colony. He was playful and was showing interest in the females, having all the sexual behaviors that frequently led the monkey male into trouble with the other males and later with the females of the colony. Fred had still to prove himself worthy of mating.

Jill was ready for the last experiment that would allow her to compare the differences in the brain function during rage while Fred was addicted to alcohol to the brain function of his normal rage reaction. She was planning to inject the isotope for the PET scan when Fred was becoming enraged. Jill was very attached to Fred; she wanted to make Fred aggressive without hurting him in any way. She would spend time playing with him even in her off hours. He was her companion when Charles was away on his soccer trips. Somehow Fred had the same effect on her that Charles had. She felt peaceful when she was with Fred in the colony.

Her moments with Charles that afternoon when she introduced Fred to Charles were so happy that those memories gave her the same wonderful feelings. She would bring a book to the colony and sit on the grass to read. Fred would immediately come to the fence and play close to her. He would bring some of his friends and hang around the area.

Jill would smile and enjoy her solitude reading and watching Fred and his buddies. Fred was a beautiful and attractive young monkey.

Jill asked Dr. Larsson, who was experienced with the monkey's behavior, "Dr. Larsson, how can I enrage Fred without physically hurting him?"

"Easy," said Dr. Larsson, "just stare into his eyes while you are 5 feet from his face."

"Don't stare in the monkey's eyes, they will become enraged. I learned that in the zoo when I was a child," said Jill laughing.

"It is true, I am not kidding," said Dr. Larsson.

"I have already stared at him, he just makes this cute face at me," said Jill.

"It is because Fred is used to you. He does not feel threatened by you, Jill. Let me show you."

Dr. Larsson stared at Fred. Fred's pupils dilated and he walked back, but he did not become enraged.

"That is not enough, Dr. Larsson. I need more reaction to completely activate his brain," said Jill.

"Well, Fred knows me. I always bring food for him when you go to San Diego. May be if you bring Charles to stare at Fred, he will react. Fred may be jealous of Charles," laughed Dr. Larsson.

"Good idea," said Jill.

Jill moved Fred from the colony to the laboratory and placed him in the cage that Charles and Roberto had built. Fred felt comfortable in this cage. Charles had already made several other improvements on it, including several toys designed to test Fred's cognition. Every time that Fred played with the toys, the computer registered his activity; it even graded the complexity of the activity depending on how intensely Fred played. Jill had noticed that since she took Fred off alcohol, he played more frequently and with more complex activities than when he was addicted. Fred now loved the toys.

That weekend, Jill brought Charles to the laboratory. They entered the room where Fred was housed, embraced each other and Jill said: "Now go and stare into Fred's eyes. Charles, stay 5 feet from him."

"Ok," said Charles and walked toward the cage.

When Charles stared at Fred, his pupils dilated. Fred stepped back and went crazy. He bolted in Charles direction and hit his face in the cage's door. Charles immediately left the room, leaving Jill alone with Fred. Jill approached the cage, talking to Fred. He put his arm through the opening in the cage and let Jill caress him. She noticed that Fred became sexually aroused. His eyes were wide and slightly teary. His pupils were midsize as he stared longingly at her. She understood then that Fred was in love with her. Her heart palpitated as a tear dropped from her eyes.

She left the room and embraced Charles.

"Oh Charles, he loves me," she said.

"Jill, he is just a monkey. What do you mean?" Charles asked.

"He gave that fit because he was jealous of you. I need to take him back to the colony soon. He needs to continue his adaptation in the colony. I am sure that he will find a mate for him there."

"Let me know what I can do to help," said Charles, understanding her concern.

"I need you here on the day of the experiment. Clearly, you have a major effect on him. He sees you as a threat to take me away from him," said Jill.

"I'll be here, even if just to make sure that Fred will not take you away from me," joked Charles, embracing her.

Jill scheduled the experiment for the first week of May. All got together in the laboratory again at 7:00 AM with doughnuts and coffee.

Dr. Hillary asked. "So, Jill, do you feel good playing the jealousy game? I thought you wanted to be a scientist and not behave like a manipulative woman."

She had described to Dr. Hillary and Dr. Mallory her plans. They were doubtful of the results but went along with Jill's experimental design. Both were experienced scientists, they knew to give opportunity to the student's ideas. Students are intelligent but naïve, still not influenced by the scientific dogma that usually delays discoveries. Dr.

Hillary was challenging Jill to entice her to defend her ideas. He was actually training her to be a good scientist. She would have to stand in front of hundreds of experts and defend her experiments; moreover, when she tried to publish her results the peer reviewers would tear her work apart.

If she were not well prepared to argue strongly for the validity of her work, she would not get her work published. It would be very difficult for her to obtain her doctorate degree in the future without the publications. The judging committees usually give great importance to a candidate that had work accepted for publication. It proved that the candidate was ready to be part of the scientific community on a very high level. Jill smiled and answered, "Professor, I am having fun. It's great to see these guys falling for me. Every woman likes to see men fighting over her."

"Really, I didn't know that. What do you feel, Jill?" asked Dr. Mallory.

"I don't know what I feel, ask the female monkeys. They let the males almost kill themselves before they pick the good one. I guess it is woman's instinct. After all, we are all primates!" said Jill.

"I hope this exercise will be helpful for our understanding of rage attacks, Jill," said Dr. Larsson and continued, "It is a lot of work to prepare these experiments. I have been working the whole week with catheters, diluting drugs, scheduling scans and making the university veterinarians happy. They are so strict these days about any experimentation in animals. The amount of paperwork is unbelievable."

"Thanks for all your work. Unfortunately, the regulations are necessary. In the past, scientists abused the animals and the society's confidence in their work. Now we have to put up with all this bureaucracy. It assures good quality work. I would rather see science delayed by the regulations than see animals being abused and bad data being collected," said Dr. Hillary.

"Bah! You are not the one doing the paperwork," answered Dr. Larsson.

"I know, but it assures good quality of science. Only groups that have it together, in all steps of the experimentation receive permission to go ahead," remarked Dr. Hillary, who had been part of the University Animal Subject Committee.

"Do you believe that people would forge scientific data?" asked Charles.

"Oh yeah! Charles, people will do anything for notoriety, power, and money!" Dr. Mallory intervened.

"Worse is that one untrue data published may delay the scientific process for decades. It will take a new experimentation to prove that publication incorrect. Moreover, it may direct other scientists in wrong lines of research, which will take them years to realize that they are on the wrong path for their discoveries. 'Lie in science is but the disgrace of the soul!' The scientist is lying to him or herself," Dr. Hillary said.

"Enough philosophy, no more doughnuts, let's work," commanded Dr. Mallory.

Jill entered Fred's room with a glass of orange juice. Fred immediately came to the front of the cage and extended his right arm to her. He picked up the glass of juice with the left hand to drink. Jill was already caressing his arm, shaving, and preparing sterile the area for puncturing of the vein. She did all this in a matter of minutes. She catheterized the vein and moved on to catheterize the artery in his wrist. She looked at Fred's face several times. Their eye contact reassured Fred of her care and judging from his calm attitude, love. When all was ready, she signaled to Dr. Larsson to bring the drugs and tell Charles to enter the room.

As Charles entered the room, Fred started to become agitated. Jill already had the isotope in the syringe triggered to inject it in Fred's vein. Charles stared at Fred's eyes for seconds. Fred was already totally out of control. Jill barely had time to inject the isotope; Fred pulled his arm from Jill and charged toward Charles. Charles went out of the room as Fred hit the cage door. The arterial catheter became loose, and blood started to spray all over. Dr. Hillary entered immediately the room and spoke, "Sedate him, Jill; you have the vein, inject propofol now."

Propofol, an anesthetic, would immediately place Fred to sleep, controlling his rage attack. Dr. Larsson however was already reducing the cage space by bringing together the walls designed to contain Fred.

He said, "Don't inject propofol, sedation with this drug will ruin the experiment. I'll inject intramuscular ketamine. It has no effect on the data because it was the anesthetic we injected in all other experiments. We have to keep it consistent."

As he injected, Jill was already being able to calm Fred down by talking to him. Dr. Hillary opened the cage as Fred became sleepy. He pressed Fred's wrist and stopped the bleeding. He looked at Jill and noticed that her eyes were teary.

He said, "Sorry Jill. I know you care about Fred. It will be all right."

"I can't do this again," she answered.

"Let's take him to the scanner. We cannot waste time, the isotope will be washed away," commanded Dr. Mallory.

"Jill, let us finish this. Go to the cafeteria with Charles and wait for us. Emotion doesn't mix well with science. You need some rest," said Dr. Hillary.

Drs. Hillary, Mallory and Larsson obtained the PET scan and brought Fred back to his cage. Fred woke up well. He was active as if nothing had happened.

Dr. Hillary said, "Fred has given us a wealth of information. It is time to bring him back to the colony and let him live his monkey life. We will need to repeat these experiments with other animals. Let's use Fred's data to apply for NIH funding. Jill's work was so outstanding that I am sure we will be able to impress them with what we can do in this laboratory. Jill will defend her Ph.D. in this subject. She will need the money to continue her studies. We will push for her to be accepted in the STAR program and get her medical and philosophy doctorate at once. This girl deserves it."

"I'll love to have her working with me, she has a spot in my lab," said Mallory.

"Great, next year she will start. Now in the end of the month we have to go to her wedding. Charles and she are marrying in Palos Verdes. Have you been in that glass church of Frank Loyd Wright?" asked Dr. Hillary.

"No, I don't have time for touring in LA. When I have time, I go to the mountains," answered Dr. Mallory.

"If you need a peaceful place in Los Angeles, go there to the glass church. The view of the Pacific and the trees you see when you are inside bring an incredible peaceful feeling. You need to learn how to enjoy Los Angeles." They left the lab and walked to the cafeteria to check on Jill.

Chapter 11
Love and Soccer

The sun was settling in the horizon, starting to form a lavender color over the Pacific. The wind coming from the ocean was mild, bouncing the tree branches softly over the glass walls of the chapel. Flute music filled the Wayfarers Chapel with simple enchantment to receive Jill. Charles, looking his best, was standing at the right side of the altar with Roberto and Chris on his right. They were a handsome trio facing the entrance of the chapel. Healthy athletes in best shape, now in preparation for the soccer World Cup; they irradiated happiness and strength to face life at its fullest. They saw Jill ready to enter the chapel; the view of the Pacific Ocean behind her gave the impression of infinite fulfillment.

Jill's smile radiated happiness and hope for a life of great achievements with Charles. When crossing the threshold of the Chapel's door, her large brown and watery eyes were emanating a love that Charles had seen before. Her beautiful white gown and dark hair over her shoulders brought to Charles memories of that night in Westwood when they merged their destiny. As they held hands in front of the altar, gazing at each other, they listened to the priest and uttered their vows to care for each other through sickness and health throughout their lives. Charles and Jill knew that sickness was the greatest challenge to the strength of their love. Both shed tears at the moment of the vows.

"What a beautiful wedding! What a setting! You are so beautiful Jill, now I understand why Fred fell so much in love with you! But the lucky man is Charlie! My wishes of a great life together," said Dr. Hillary as he complimented the newlyweds outside the chapel.

"So, where is the honeymoon?" asked Dr. Mallory, who was just after Dr. Hillary in the reception line.

"No honeymoon at this time, I start working Monday. World Soccer Cup starts in less than a month!" answered Charles.

"Not easy being a wife of a soccer player," joked Jill.

Indeed, the honeymoon was cut short; there was little time for celebration. They had a small reception outside the chapel, enjoying the end of the sunset and the incredibly beautiful view of the Palos Verdes Mountains against the Pacific. They rested the next day and Charles was the taken to training camp in Gardena. He was to spend the next 45 days in complete seclusion and training if the USA team was to be successful. Charles accepted the idea of spending all this time without seeing Jill just because he was living one of the dreams of his life, to play soccer for his country. The experience of playing against the most awesome soccer players in the world gave him an incredible thrill. He had great hope of beating teams like Argentina, Brazil, Italy, Germany, and England.

The best of 32 rounds of games was scheduled to start in June. The USA team's opening was against Italy, the defending champions. Obviously, Italy was the favorite, although Charles', Roberto's and Chris' names were starting to appear in the media, especially in the Spanish speaking American media. They were not a match, however against the famous European soccer stars. Nonetheless, the Americans had great hope in their young trio. They were starting to get contracts for advertisement; their financial life was promising to improve fast, especially if they managed to get to the finals.

Jill phoned Charles three days before the game against Italy.

"Charlie, I miss you! Are you prepared for the Italians?"

"I miss you too, Jill. I want to offer this first game to you and to our marriage."

"Thanks dear, I know you will do well. Be careful with the Italians, they can be aggressive, control yourself. I don't want to see you out of the game without showing them the best of your soccer!"

"Don't worry, dear; the coaches have drilled into me the need to be calm and not to risk my position in the initial phase of the tournament. There is a whole scheme designed to keep me away from direct confrontation. We are playing a very fast passing game. Roberto, Chris and I never played so well together. It is like playing music; our movements are perfect. I am confident that we will beat the Italians. They are having problems. They have too many stars; they are not able to work together as a team, at least at the level we are. I am sure we will do well. We have rehearsed several plays that you will love. Watch the game with Roberto's dad. He will help you understand it."

"Roberto's, my parents and your parents will watch the games together," said Jill.

"Great, I've got to go, it is time to go to bed; the schedule here is very strict. Love you, miss you, goodnight."

"Love you too, keep up the good spirits, we are praying for you."

The Italians were really not ready to play against the USA. Although they had more skilled players, the unity was not there. The USA team closed up their defense and Charles was able to open up the score in the first half. They won 1 to 0. The Italians couldn't believe it. They were not out of the tournament yet. The USA team, however, was well on its way to make to the best of 16. USA won the next two games and tied the last game of this phase with Germany. Both went ahead to the best of 16 rounds, Italy was knocked out. Charles had one yellow card that he received during the game against Germany. Roberto was able to get to him and grab him when things were getting out of control against the German sweeper who had tripped him; however, he still received the yellow card.

Charles had scored three goals in this first round. America was thrilled with his performance, so was Coach Pirelli who was the assistant coach of the American team. Pirelli was proud of what he had accomplished with Charles; he had accepted however that he was not able to teach Charles to control his temper. Besides training Roberto and Chris to interfere promptly when Charles lacked self-control, Coach Pirelli could just hope for the best, as it had happened over the past two years of Charles' professional soccer tenure.

Competition intensified, now one loss and the team would be out. The USA moved forward again winning 1 to 0 against England, a completely unexpected result. Charles completed the goal after a perfect pass from Chris. They now had to face Brazil to go to the finals. The Brazilians had won all the games they had played. They knew by now already the strengths and weaknesses of the American team, including Charles' volatility. At this level of competition, all weaknesses of the opponent team would be exploited to its fullest. The experienced Brazilian professional players knew how to irritate a player and psychologically disarm him. Coach Pirelli advised Charles of this and of the shrewdness of the Brazilian sweeper.

The game was scheduled for Fourth of July in the Rose Bowl in Pasadena, California.

The stadium was beautiful and filled to capacity. Jill was there with her parents, Charles' parents and Roberto's parents. They had excellent seats together with the American dignitaries present for this celebration. Although soccer was not the preferred sport for the majority of Americans, its importance in the world and the performance of the American team had gained national attention. Charles was already recognized as the hero of the games. Although the Americans had won always with a low score, Charles was instrumental in all of them. It was well understood the level of competition they were facing and pride had risen in the heart of the Americans.

This game, played on the Fourth of July, took even greater nationalistic proportion. The game would start at 4 PM and be followed by fireworks. Charles was under incredible pressure to perform. The nation's eyes were on him. Jill was anxious and rightly so; she knew how much pressure Charles could take. She held Charles' mother's hand, and both prayed for his calm and success.

The coach of the American team fired them up in the locker room. "Remember guys, the Brazilian team is the toughest team in this tournament. They are together, they have incredible players, but they are no match for us. Our defense is the best of the tournament, Chris and Roberto are dominating in the midfield and Charles is faster than their sweeper. We have to rely on the wings to bring the ball to the end zone and send it back to Chris and Roberto; they will find Charles in the box. Chris and Roberto, when you serve a ball to Charles, one follows him closely for the rebound and the other make yourself available for Charles to pass it to you if he needs so. Charles, control yourself, we can win this game!"

The Rose Bowl never saw so many American flags. There was a small section of Brazilians comprising less than 10% of the audience. All nationalities were present but approximately 80% of the 100,000 people were in American colors. It was a red, white and blue party. The colors, the music and the excitement at the stadium were unprecedented, even in major American football games. The game started after the national anthems were played. Initially the Brazilians dominated the game. Their fast passing and skills were clearly superior to the American team. However, the Americans were fired up by nationalism. Their defense was seamless; the Brazilians could not break it in the first half. Neither could the Americans perform their planned strategy. Two outstanding Brazilian halfbacks were blocking the American wing attacks. Roberto and Chris were having difficulty negotiating the ball in the midfield. Charles often found himself dribbling toward the key alone, facing the skilled Brazilian sweeper and goalkeeper with no chance of a clean shot at the goal.

This was a difficult game. The strategies decided during the resting period would certainly define the game. Both teams had studied each other carefully in the first half; the best coaching in either side would likely decide the outcome. As assistant coach, Pirelli advised the American coach to use Charles to decide the game. They had to bring Charles back to carry the ball from the midfield, instead of waiting for it in the box. Roberto and Chris clearly could not detangle the midfield, and the Brazilians had incredible control of the ball. This strategy would increase the risk of Charles' direct confrontation with the Brazilian defense; the Americans, however, did not have another choice. The major risk was that Charles would break through the defense alone because of his great speed. Roberto or Chris would not be able to follow him closely. Hopefully, he would be able to avoid a fight.

The second half started with the stadium encouraging Charles to score. His name was heard in unison, and he was fired up. Ten minutes into the second half Charles received the ball in the midfield from the American sweeper. He cleared the first line of defense and was faced with the sweeper. Roberto and Chris were running from the defense to help Charles, but he was at least twenty yards ahead. He sped and faced the Brazilian sweeper that had much irritated Charles in the first half of the game. Charles dribbled past without difficulty and became face to face with the goalkeeper, just outside of the box. The Brazilian sweeper sped after Charles, but Charles was too fast for him, so he jumped and embraced Charles from behind as Charles was preparing to place the ball in the corner of the Brazilian's goal. Charles placed all the violence intended for the kick in his elbow, hitting the forehead of the sweeper, who fell convulsing on the grass. Charles placed the ball into the goal.

He received an immediate red card and was expelled from the game. Charles attempted to run after the referee, however, Roberto had already arrived to hold him and calm him down. The Brazilian sweeper was taken from the field on a stretcher and was transferred unconscious to a hospital. The referee annulled the goal but gave the Americans a free kick in goal since the Brazilian committed the initial foul. Roberto scored with a perfect kick that hit the post and entered the goal. The Brazilians equaled the score with an Olympic goal kicked from the left corner and finally won the game after the overtime in penalty kicks.

The Brazilian sweeper had a large skull fracture with an epidural hematoma, bleeding outside the covers of the brain. The pressure over the brain was released with an operation and the player stayed in the hospital a full week before being transferred to the rehabilitation unit. Charles became very depressed. He decided that this was the end of his soccer career. Coach Pirelli convinced him to accept several offers for advertisement of sports merchandise. This would help him to build the necessary financial reserve to support him and Jill through the school years.

Jill supported his decision; she was sad that Charles could not taste the glory he deserved for his outstanding soccer abilities. He was deprived because of his lack of self-control. She had to help him. She was motivated more than ever before of achieving her goal of becoming a neurosurgeon and scientist.

Chapter 12
Newlyweds

Charles returned home from the games in severe depression. He felt guilty for the loss of the American soccer team. He could not accept how he let down his teammates and the whole nation. He blamed himself for not being there to play in the overtime and moreover, the American goalkeeper had to kick one of the penalty kicks, the very one that was missed. If he was there, he would have kicked and made the goal; he rarely missed those. Charles lost interest in life in general; he was even cold toward Jill. She could not understand.

"Charlie, you have to shake this off! You are the only one who thinks that you were the cause of the American loss. The whole stadium was in awe with your soccer abilities. The loss was just bad luck. The Brazilians never did win the game, it was a penalty kick fluke, could happen with any team," said Jill.

"I wouldn't have missed that kick and I probably would have scored in the overtime. I had just figured out how to beat that sweeper."

"He irritated you too much, Charlie. I noticed he was always kicking and pushing you, even when you were not with the ball," said Jill.

"I couldn't take it anymore, what an unfair grab he made. What an unfair red card I received! I had to control myself though. The coaches warned me about him."

"Charlie, forget it! We have to move on. Your advertisement contracts need to be fulfilled. We need the money, this is your only chance to take advantage of all the effort you put in soccer. This is a short lived thing, in few months or weeks everybody will forget the World Cup and we won't have money to complete our studies," insisted Jill impatiently.

"Who wants to listen to the advice of a loser like me? On the top of that, I destroyed the life of that sweeper, he is not able to play and probably never will. He had a huge brain surgery."

"Charlie, please let this pass. You are being too hard on yourself. The whole stadium continued shouting your name in unison, even after the American loss. They love you and they want to listen to you. The sports comments after the game were all accolades to you. You are a hero for this nation; let's use it in our advantage. Next week, you have an advertisement audition. You need to be at your best. I'll help you," said Jill, lovingly.

"Thanks Jill. I don't feel like it though, do you think I can perform. What is it about? Have you read the script?"

"Sure I did, it is about the toughness of Nike shin guard. They are paying us $50,000. It is what we need to complete our down payment for a flat here in Westwood. You have to get it," explained Jill.

"What do I have to say?"

"You just have to say that the Nike shin guard kept you in the game almost to the end and that you didn't have a single bruise on your shin. That is easy, because you didn't. The guard really did protect you because that guy kicked your legs all the time!" Jill joked.

Charles was still negative about it. Jill was losing her patience. They needed the money bad. They had at least 7 to 8 years of school ahead of them. The salary of a grad student was meager, if any. Medical students make nothing, just expenses. She was getting desperate. Their savings would keep them, as it is, no more than 2 years. She would not start making money as a resident for the next 5 years. She had to rely on Charles to put her through grad and medical school. Charles did not seem to see that far. She finally broke down.

"Charlie, you need help. I cannot cheer you up anymore. I believe you need medication. School will not start until mid-September; we have a month to get you out of this and make some money. Let's see Dr. Hillary and your psychiatrist. Medication may be helpful here, at least to take you out of this depression. What do you think?"

"You know best, Jill. I will do whatever you want," said an apathetic Charles.

"I'll talk with Dr. Hillary today and set a consult with the psychiatrist tomorrow," said Jill.

It was 11 AM; he closed his eyes and dozed off. Jill picked up the phone and called Dr. Hillary's office. The secretary answered.

"May I speak with Dr. Hillary?" asked Jill.

"He is in surgery until one, do you want to leave a message?"

"Tell him that Jill called and asked to have an urgent conversation with him. I will be waiting for his call in my home," said Jill.

"Will do!"

Dr. Hillary called before one.

"Hey Jill! What is up, too much fun in the honeymoon? You want to share it with me?" Dr. Hillary joked.

"Dr. Hillary, I really need your help. Things are not easy here. Charlie has not bounced back from the soccer loss. He is completely apathetic. I need him ready for auditions and school is coming. I don't know what to do," said Jill.

"Bring Charlie. I will meet you at Jerry's Deli in 30 minutes," said Dr. Hillary.

***

"Charlie, what is up?" asked Dr. Hillary a few minutes later in a small restaurant close to the hospital.

"That moment that I hit the Brazilian sweeper does not leave my mind. It looks like I have a closed circuit in my brain, it is driving me crazy. I cannot concentrate on anything else!" said Charles.

"What about concentrating on this beautiful wife of yours?" Dr. Hillary asked.

"I try, I am not being fair with her, but that game keeps on taking my brain over. I think Jill is right, I need some help. Do you think that medication will do it?" asked Charles, almost pleading.

"Sure, it will. You are correct, Charles. You have a closed circuit in your brain. We all do. Papez described this in the 1930s. It is called the limbic system. Some have more control of it than others. You clearly have poor control of yours. There are drugs that break the cycle. You should take one of them for a while. Serotonin re-uptake inhibitors are great; it will begin to work in about one week. Time enough for you to go through your audition. Then when school starts, we will evaluate if you have side-effects and make other decisions. Let's start it today, I will prescribe. Tomorrow, you see your psychiatrist. I will call and inform him of our decision."

"Thanks, Dr. Hillary," said Jill.

"Charlie, the ideal would be if we could turn on a switch and stop your reverberating circuitry. I believe we can do it with a simple electric current through one of the relays of the limbic system," Dr. Hillary said.

"Why don't we do it?" Charles asked anxiously.

"Science is not quite ready for it. This is part of the research that you and Jill will do. Charles, we will have lots of fun in the next 10 years. I will love working with you. Cheer up, I want to see you in one week," said Dr. Hillary as he stood up and walked back to the hospital.

***

Although sleeping 12 hours per day, Charles bounced back. He prepared for the audition; he aced it and got the money that they so much needed. Jill was grateful to him. This would hold them for two more years, time for her to start making some money, maybe writing a grant, and getting a young investigator award, or even using the intern salary. Well, this was way in the future. They would manage. Jill knew, however, that Charles could not do well as a grad student sleeping 12 hours per day. Some adjustments of his medication needed to be done.

She was convinced that Charles should try medication now for an extended period of time; this would be in preparation for a possible surgery in the future. He no longer had the demand of soccer, and the beginning of grad school should not be too difficult for him. She needed him functioning at least on an independent level. It was too emotionally taxing to serve as his cheering up person. The conversations with him when he was depressed were laborious and long. He was so negative; she had to use increasingly complex arguments to cheer him up. She usually was drained after those conversations.

Moreover, on the current medication, their sex life was poor. She feared for their relationship. He was getting frustrated with himself, and many times he was impatient with her. Charlie was doing marginally in his course work. He had to get better grades; otherwise, he would lose his candidacy for his philosophy doctorate.

***

"Charlie, it has been three months now that you have been on this medication. What do you think?"

"I want to stop it. I am no longer depressed, I need to be sharper, and I cannot continue sleeping my head off. What do we do?"

"Hey, let's stop it. I fell in love with you on no medication. I like you better without it. I believe we can cheer ourselves up. Let's advise your doctor of what we want to do," said Jill.

So, they did. Charles returned to his cheerful and bright mood. He had taken the World Cup game off his mind. Now his brain was full of excitement with his research. He was learning in depth the circuitry of the brain and the electrophysiology necessary to manipulate the system. Next year he was scheduled to work in a laboratory dedicated to nano-electronic devices. During this year, their marriage blossomed. Charles was witty and a great lover. It was the last year of Jill's undergrad school and, although busy, she had time to spend with him. They were experiencing a blessed life.

Chapter 13
Life Multiplying

Charles came home from UCLA and Jill was in her 'power white dress'. There was no dinner waiting for him, although she had some candles lit.

"Dear, what are you trying to tell me?" He asked, embracing her.

"I want to take you out for dinner. I have a gift for you."

"What is it?" It was not close to his birthday; he couldn't think of any special occasion.

"I'll tell you later on; take a shower and dress up. I will pour some wine for you; I don't want to have it. Relax, we will have a great night," said Jill, touching his nose with her index finger and kissing his cheek.

"Are we driving or walking? I don't want to drink if we are driving," said Charles.

"We walk, I have reservations close by. The night feels great and the moon is full. I want to enjoy you," she said.

"What is up with you? It is Tuesday, I have a full day tomorrow," insisted Charles as he undressed for his shower.

"Wait, you will love it. Tomorrow you will manage. We will have tougher nights ahead of us. You will see," she hinted.

They went to a small fancy restaurant and sat in a corner table with two lit candles and a starched white tablecloth. She was beautiful and her eyes were large and bright, with that teary look that she always got when she was overcome by love. She held both of his hands across the table and said: "Charlie, I am pregnant."

"Wow, now we have our hands full. Now I understand why you didn't want to have wine and why our nights will get tougher. You are right; we are in for a big mess. I want to kiss you all over. I love you. I-I…how will we manage baby, grad school, hospital, surgery? Are you sure that we can have a baby? I thought you were on the pill. You told me you were."

"Yes, I was. I missed two days last month. You have been hot lately. Since you got off medication, you returned to your stud self; I can barely keep up with you. Looks like you are putting all your soccer energy on me. Now is time to take a break," she said smiling.

"No breaks, I want you tonight. We need to commemorate. You know I cannot control my instincts when you are wearing this dress. I know you have bad intentions tonight," he said, squeezing her hands gently.

"You bet I do. Charlie, I love you. We will manage the baby. We are not the first grad students that have to deal with child rearing during school. My mom and your mom can help. They are close by. The baby will be so beautiful; he will look like you."

"How do you know it is he?"

"I don't know. It just feels to be so. I already love the baby, and you are the only image that I have of how he or she will look. It is easy to think of it as a man. It really doesn't matter. What do you prefer?"

"I prefer a girl with dark eyes and dark hair. I love you," he said touching her nose. She smiled, held and kissed his finger.

"Oh, Charlie, I am so happy!"

He raised his wine glass and drank a sip looking deep in her eyes.

"What a full life you are providing me. I am the luckiest man in the world. Did you tell this to anybody else?"

"No, I only told you. Tomorrow we will tell our parents and Dr. Hillary. They will be happy, you will see," she said.

"I believe Dr. Hillary will be worried. He expects so much work from us," said Charles.

"I doubt he will. Let's see what he says."

They finished dinner, walked back home slowly, and had a peaceful night in each other's arms.

Chapter 14
Voxel

Jill had a hard time adapting to pregnancy. Nausea dominated the initial 3 months; during this period, Charles was very supportive. He started to help her with her computer work in the laboratory. She took advantage of every minute she had off from her undergrad work to further her brain research. She needed to match voxel by voxel of the images of Fred's brain detecting differences while he was in addiction, rage and at rest. She had an enormous database to analyze. She needed computer expertise, which Charles could provide.

"Dr. Mallory asked me to compare voxel by voxel of the images of Fred's brain. I have no idea what a voxel is. Do you know what it is, Charlie?"

"Sure, I do. A voxel is a volumetric computer unit of an image. In your case, it is a virtual unit of Fred's brain. As you have images acquired with different techniques in different states of Fred's brain, you can compare these virtual volumes bit by bit as Dr. Mallory asked you to do. It is simple, no? Do you need help?"

"I have no idea how to start," answered Jill.

"Did Dr. Mallory explain to you how?"

"Charlie, he has no idea how to do it himself. He told me that it is part of my doctorate research to figure stuff like this out. He just told me to go ask for help from the people of the advanced radiology center for imaging in the hospital. I don't know who they are."

"Dr. Mallory was helpful. At least he told you where to ask. My advisor wouldn't even give that much of a hint. He wants you to learn how to find all the answers yourself; he says it is part of the training as a scientist. Jill, I want to go there with you. You have a fascinating project!" said Charles.

"Thanks, Charlie. Being with you turns work into fun. It's nice to have you translating the computer jargon for me. When I talk with computer guys, I have a blank in my mind. They are so much into their dot coms, dot orgs, pixels, voxels, jpegs, and tiff files that I end up just nodding my head in agreement with their babble," said Jill laughing.

"Jill, it is not that complicated. Just think of our baby. It is growing cell by cell. Each cell can be compared to a voxel in one of Fred's brain images. They have different function to a point of making a whole human being. Same with your image, each voxel is representing a virtual state of function and together will form a complete brain. Voxels will be detected differently depending on the imaging technique used."

"For example: Xray computed tomography (CT) detects voxels depending on the attenuation of the tissue to x-rays. It does not detect function, only attenuation, giving only anatomic information of the brain. Magnetic Resonance (MRI) detects the state of activation of water in the tissue; it can give excellent anatomical definition, but also function if the activation is manipulated by changing the electromagnetic field around the patient's head. Positron Emission Tomography (PET) builds voxels based on energy emitted by radioactive molecules injected in the blood stream and captured by specific cells in the brain, depending on their function at the moment of injection."

"You have also the magnetoencephalography in your project. It builds voxels based on the electric state of the brain regions. I guess I am complicating this too much. Let's go to the imaging laboratory, I'll explain these things to you as we go along in your research."

"Wow Charlie, you know so much! Where did you learn all this?" asked Jill.

"Biological imaging is a class required in one of my coursework, I'm just in the midst of studying this. It's exciting to have the chance to work with it on a practical level. It seems to me that we will have to write some computer program to put all this together. I can help you with it," said Charles.

"I love you, brainy guy!"

"I love you too, brainy girl! Let's go!"

They arrived in this room full of huge computer monitors with people hunched in front of them. It took a while for them to get the attention of one of the guys. They explained what they needed. The guy just said: "Return next week. We have a grant application due this Friday, nobody has time for students this week. We will be glad to help you then. See you."

"Thanks, we will return next week then," said Charles.

"They are not very friendly," said Jill.

"Don't worry, computer guys are like this, no social skills. However, they love to show what they do. They face a real deadline. If they don't get funded, they all lose their jobs. It is too cutthroat at the university. They are all in what is called soft money; their salaries come from grants or grateful patient donations to people like Dr. Hillary. It is the same with us graduate students," said Charles.

"Great, I need a break anyway. Terms are close and I have to study. I need high grades to make it into medical school. I'll take the M-CATS soon. I have to prepare myself."

"Don't push too much. You know, the baby," said Charles.

"Well, I have to do it. The baby will just grow up brainy like you," she joked.

Chapter 15
More Science

Charles, Jill and Drs Hillary, Mallory and Larsson met to discuss voxels. It was time for the grant application. The deadline was in one month. They needed to show some of the data obtained in Fred's experiments as an initial demonstration that the laboratory could conduct imaging research of a high complexity level. Dr. Mallory was relying on Jill's initial analyses of the PET and MRI scans. This was crucial because it was the first time that the laboratory got involved in such high level imaging analyses. The laboratory was well known for the research in addiction, behavior, and pharmacology. Imaging was a completely new ball game. They had no tradition in the field. Except for Dr. Hillary's neurosurgical understanding of images of the brain, the group had no computer expertise in imaging analyses. This grant would hinge in the shoulders of Jill and Charles, using the recognized names of Drs Hillary, Mallory, and Larsson.

"Peter, how would you design the experiments for the grant application?" Dr. Mallory asked Dr. Hillary.

"Ask Jill; I would do just what she did with Fred. She has to find a way to expedite the process. We have to study at least 6 animals in each group to obtain statistical confirmation of the findings. I also think that we should study the MRI and PET of naturally aggressive animals to compare with the data we obtain on the aggressive behavior when the animal becomes jealous. It may be that the brain nuclei and pathways involved are different in the naturally aggressive animal," answered Dr. Hillary.

"What do you think, Jill?" asked Dr. Mallory.

"Dr. Hillary is correct. We have to expedite the process. This is the issue! Do you think that me or any other person preparing the monkeys for the image studies will be able to get their confidence and make them fall in love in a short period of time? Do you think the reviewers will buy the story of monkeys loving humans and becoming jealous to the point of becoming aggressive?" asked Jill.

"I have an idea," advanced Dr. Larsson. "Why don't we further condition the natural reaction that the monkey has of getting upset when someone stares in his eyes? This can easily be done with the stare followed by an uncomfortable stimulation, such as a light electrical shock. Charles could prepare the experimental cage so that a light electrical current could pass through the floor, giving the animal a slight jolt just during the stare."

"Great, this sounds scientific. We can quantify the electrical current almost to manipulate the intensity of the reaction. Also, we can be sure that the animal is not feeling pain. We have to take advantage of the summation of stimuli, the staring and the electrical shock. Can you do this?" asked Dr. Mallory to Charles.

"Sure, control of the electrical current through the floor of the cage shouldn't be a problem. It will depend on Jill to generate the staring reaction," answered Charles.

"No," said Jill. "You are the staring professional. Fred went bonkers when you stared at him. I think you should be responsible for the whole thing since you can quantify your staring and the electrical current. You also have to prove that the electrical current is not causing pain to the animal. In other words, when there is no staring, the animal should only turn off a switch to stop the current, as if to terminate some uncomfortable feeling. They are so smart; I can teach them to do that easily," Jill said.

"Great Jill, put this on paper. We have to start writing immediately. I will write all the background of the research and complete review of the animal behavioral, rage and imaging literature. Jill will write the Materials and Methods of the study. Jill, all the procedures we did in Fred's experiments should be carefully detailed. I will help you. Charles, you need to write a complete description of the cage. The electrical circuit in particular; prove that it is safe, comfortable for the monkey and reliable in the data generation. I will ask Jorgen to write the complete review on monkey alcohol addiction. Jorgen, could you do that?" asked Dr. Mallory to Dr. Larsson.

"Sure, it will also be a pleasure to help Jill and Charles if they need it," answered Dr. Larsson.

"I will write the significance of the experiments to the human situation. I will also review the imaging literature related to rage. There is quite a bit now on the importance of the frontal lobes in behavioral studies using PET. It is actually very interesting literature. Jill and Charles, let me know if you need help," said Dr. Hillary.

"Great, sounds like we have a plan. It is missing only one important piece of the application. The pilot data section! Have you and Charles found any interesting data on the voxel story?" asked Dr. Mallory.

"We were postponed," answered Jill. "The guys at the advanced imaging laboratory didn't want to talk with us. Their grant is due this week. They will talk with us on Monday. Charles and I will be on top of it. Charles actually has quite a bit of understanding on the subject. He is just now studying imaging in his course work," said Jill.

"Jill, the pilot data is the most important part of this whole application, the NIH reviewers will not give us the money if we don't prove to them that we can do the experiments. It will be great if we find something interesting in the data. Then the application will be even more compelling. We need to see some results by the end of next week. Good luck, you two," said Dr. Mallory.

"We need to meet again the end of next week. Each one should bring they have written. We need to give Dr. Mallory the digital texts so he can piece the thing together. He is very good at it. Remember, the literature reviews need to be complete. Charles and Jill, your descriptions of the experimental design need to be backed up by the literature. You have to go read on methods of monkey behavior research, as well as cage construction. All this has been done in the past. Charles, you need to write also about the methods of image analysis and the computer hardware necessary. We need to put a budget together; this is an important part of the grant application. Good luck to all!" said Dr. Hillary.

Dr. Hillary invited Charles and Jill for lunch. He needed to talk with them further. Charles and Jill felt under pressure. A lot of work was asked from them. They had no idea how long it would take them to analyze Fred's data. Moreover, the review of the literature would not be easy either. Jill had to finish her terms and Charles also. Jill also needed to have good hours of sleep because of the pregnancy. They divided the work so that Charles would go to the library and gather all the reading material necessary. Jill would study for her test this Friday.

Charles also had a test on Friday, but he was prepared, and his grades were not as crucial as Jill's; he was already in grad school. Jill was depending on the grades to enter medical school. They would do the writing during the weekend and the data analysis during the week with the guys from the advanced imaging center.

Chapter 16
Bundle of Love

"Are you two all right? I noticed that you were exchanging looks when Dr. Mallory gave your tasks. Is it too much?" asked Dr. Hillary when they sat for lunch.

"We don't know if it is too much because we don't have any idea how long it will take to analyze Fred's data. Jill is in her terms; I also have to do mine. I believe we can manage but we are worried. We also have something else to tell you. We planned to tell you a long time ago, but we haven't had any private moment with you. I want Jill to say it." Charles looked to Jill.

"Dr. Hillary, I don't know how you will take this. We are worried that you will think that we will be too busy to work in our project or that we are not serious about our commitment with our studies, but I am pregnant," Jill said.

"What does love have to do with it, as Tina Turner says? Work and have a baby; it will be daunting, but it will bring the best of you. You will manage it; you are full of energy and young. Sleep can always be postponed to the moment that you fall asleep standing. Your body's physiology will take care of it," said Dr. Hillary.

"You really think that the baby will not add a whole new layer of work that is even more demanding than science and school?" asked Charles.

"Sure it will, but the baby is part of the two of you, you will take care of it as you take care of yourselves. You will share responsibility, cover for each other at work, help each other in the projects; actually, I believe that the baby will help your relationship. You will be obliged to depend deeply on each other. This 'bundle of love' will link your lives because you will have to maintain the 'bundle' with your love. The pressure to perform because now you are responsible for this new life will increase; you will become better workers, more mature and more productive. I have to congratulate you for this important step in your maturity as adults. Please let me know what I can do to help you through fatherhood Charles. Sorry I cannot help you, Jill; I have never been pregnant!" laughed Dr. Hillary.

"Thank you for the support, we have not thought of it in these terms. Even though we are happy, we are also scared with the amount of work that is coming in our direction," said Jill.

"It is part of being married. As soon as one gets married, hell breaks loose. It depends on the attitude of the couple. If there is friendship and mutual responsibility, if both are mature and unselfish, if the preoccupation of each is the comfort and happiness of the other and not how little one can pitch in, so ones' comfort and interests are not sacrificed, all goes well. Couples tend to grow and become successful faster when the children are born," said Dr. Hillary.

"Lots of people would disagree with you, Dr. Hillary," said Jill.

"Lots of people have children without being mature. They resent the child or children because they were not strong enough to follow their own dreams. They use the children as their excuse for their professional failure. The children grow resenting the parents or feeling guilty because of the constant complaints of how much of a burden they were through life. That is why we have so many people depending on Psychologists to find out why they hate their parents. Why do they feel so guilty? Why are they not able to love? It is because their parents didn't really transmit love to them. They transmitted only resentment. It is a major problem of the current society that presses man and woman to be outstanding professionals and perfect parents at the same time," said Dr. Hillary.

"Well, Dr. Hillary, you are asking just this from us," said Jill.

"You bet I am. I am because I believe in your love. You have proven it to me. Jill, you will have hard times and Charles will also, but fortunately these hard times usually will not come together. Charles will be there for you when you need him, and you will be there for him when he needs you. When it is hard for both, ask for help from the people you know that love you, including me. Think of your parents and friends like Roberto and Chris."

"These are all people with their own problems; however, if you rotate your friends and make new ones throughout your lives, then the burden can be spread to a great number of people that for sure will need your help in the future. You are preparing yourselves to be very valuable people. Doctors and engineers are very important assets to society. You have incredible potential to pay back the help you will receive, even though the ones that helped you with true love, will never expect to be repaid," said Dr. Hillary.

"Thanks, Dr. Hillary," said Charles.

"Really, thanks," said Jill.

"Sorry I monopolized our conversation with my cheap philosophy. You needed to hear it though. Don't worry; we are all here for you. You young people receive from the mature people like me what will be given in the future to the young people that will come after you. It is the cycle of life! Got to go! I have a surgery at one. Bye!" said Dr. Hillary, leaving them alone in the restaurant.

"Bundle of love, I never thought of the baby like a bundle of love. I guess Dr. Hillary is right. The baby started out with a seed of your love and my love, now this love is multiplying cell by cell into a bundle of cells, each one being a unit of our love and together making a bundle. It actually sounds scientific, like your voxel story, Charlie," said Jill.

"Jill, you are becoming romantic with science. You remember Dr. Hillary saying that feelings don't mix well with science, or vice versa. Do you remember the day that Fred had that fit of love and jealousy for you?" said Charles.

"Charlie, thanks for reminding me of Fred; I want to go to the colony to find out how his adaptation is advancing. I bet you he has a girlfriend," said Jill.

"I bet you she is already pregnant like you," said Charles, laughing.

"If she is pregnant, he must be hurting everywhere, because a bunch of females probably beat him up good. I am worried about what he has to go through," said Jill.

"Come on, Jill, he would love to let you beat him up so he could be with you. He let you stick needles in him. Probably he did that because instinctively he was prepared to bare pain to get love. I am sure you didn't forget how much Fred loves you," said Charles.

"That is why I worry about him. I also love him. He was always so special. He was always there for me when you were on your soccer trips. Charlie, he was my best friend for three years. I still have fond memories of being close to the fence, listening to the waterfall, reading or thinking about you. Fred spent all of his time close to the fence when I was there, looking at me and playing with his friends around me, always entertaining me away of how much I missed you. What a special guy. I wonder if he would come close to the fence again if I show up in the colony. I will try one day," said Jill.

"Go there before your belly gets big, so you will not break his heart," said Charles, laughing.

"Charlie, don't push it. Let's go back to the library; we have a lot of work to do."

Chapter 17
Student Salary

Charles and Jill slept very little that week. They managed to analyze Fred's data. The 'nerds' at the computer laboratory were not able to help them. Charles and Jill returned to Dr. Hillary and asked what to do.

"Easy," Dr. Hillary said. "Why didn't you talk with me earlier? I have a group of people that can help you. Dr. Mallory doesn't know about the clinical facilities. We manipulate images all the time for surgery. You can talk with my medical physicists or with my bioengineer, both have the software that will put Fred's images together and allow you analyze them as necessary. Actually, when the experiments were designed, I had already planned how to manipulate the data and extract the information. You don't have enough time to put the data together and learn enough of the imaging literature to include this information in the grant application before the deadline."

"Don't worry. Please try to identify differences in the diverse state of Fred's brain. For the grant application, I believe it is enough to show the NIH reviewers that we can detect differences. We need to show that our techniques are reliable and that our hypothesis can be answered with the techniques available to us. They understand that these are laborious experiments, extremely difficult to understand and very expensive. They will also understand the importance of the success of these studies in order to improve the quality of life of millions of people with severe psychiatric diseases," said Dr. Hillary.

"Who shall I ask for help first?" asked Charles.

"Go talk with the medical physicists first. They are outstanding in computers and have deep understanding of medical problems. The ones that work with me have great knowledge of brain anatomy and function. They will be able to help and teach you."

"Do they know brain electrophysiology? We also need to deal with the magnetoencephalography data," asked Jill.

"You will have to ask the bioengineer to help you with MEG data. He has the same software for imaging analysis used by the medical physicists. Charles will be able to cross information and you two will make the bridge between their knowledge. Good luck!" Dr. Hilary said.

"They were able to put the analysis together and write their part of the application in time to meet with the group at the end of the week. Dr. Mallory was astonished with the amount of work they accomplished. There were amazing differences between the images of Fred's brain in the different states of his mood. The group speculated the causes but nothing was concrete. They used the data and the pictures generated and the application was sent on time to the National Institute of Mental Health. They asked for 5 million dollars to be paid during the period of 5 years. Included on the budget were salaries for Jill and Charles as graduate students," Dr. Hillary said:

"If we get funded, you will have your next 5 years of studies secure. You will work like a dog, but you want to be a scientist and a physician; it will be just the training you need to be able to work like a dog the rest of your lives. One thing I can assure you, you will have so much fun in the process that you will never worry very much about the money you are making. Money will always be enough for you just because you will never have time to spend it.

Society will give back to you what you are giving to society. I would love to work with you over the next years. You are so capable!"

"I have never before worked with students at your level so able to create and digest information. Looks like your brains are completely wired up together. I hope that each half of your baby's brain comes from each of you," said Dr. Mallory, laughing.

"Charles and Jill, I want to invite you for dinner at my home. We have to commemorate your help in the grant application and your pregnancy," said Dr. Larsson.

"I have to tell you, what we did this past 3 weeks is much more exciting than playing soccer in the World Cup. It is a completely different level of accomplishment. It is so exciting to look at the brain images and feel you are inside of this incredibly perfect computer. It is wired in a way that man will never be able to reconstruct something similar," said Charles.

"You are correct, Charles. I just wish we had a way to access the relay that controls people's anxiety, aggressiveness, compulsion, and depression without changing the make-up of their mental essence."

"Do you really think this is possible?" asked Charles.

"That's why I am asking for your help," answered Dr. Hillary and continued in his excitement, "The interface of micro devices with the micro circuitry of the brain will be an accomplishment that will improve the lives of millions of people, not only for the patients, but also for the victims of these patients. Entire families are destroyed by cycling moods, such as in manic-depressive disorders, careers are destroyed due to premenstrual syndrome, people become psychiatric invalids due to obsessive compulsive disorder and millions commit suicide due to severe and refractory depression. These diseases can be modulated by proper electrical impulses delivered on demand by the patient's brain as it enters the state of imbalance."

"How do you think that patients will accept to be controlled by an electrical device?" interrupted Charles.

"Obviously, the patients need to have complete control of these electrical impulses and accept their triggering only when it is of their volition. We have the technology for this type of therapy; we only need to organize the devices, images, patient's diagnostic patterns and develop the necessary knowledge and education of physicians to offer this therapy for those who suffer," answered Dr. Hillary and continued, "This grant is the first step in this complex task. What I just said I wrote in a very compelling way in the Clinical Relevance Justification of the grant application. I am so excited with the possibility of doing this study, mainly because I know that Charles and Jill demonstrated passion and are committed to write their doctorate in this subject. I will do everything in my power to provide this group with the environment necessary for intellectual flourishing to bring our dream to reality. I am very thankful to all in the group for the effort of the past two years, I am sure that our payoff is in the near future."

"What a speech, I would fund you immediately! I just know that the reviewers will find a way to criticize the study. Unfortunately, many times they require that you give them all the answers before they give you the money. I have been excited with many grant applications in the past just to receive a poor review score," said Dr. Mallory.

"That is why we need to continue analyzing the data, Jill and Charles. Now that we have the software issues worked out, you should try to analyze all the details of your notes on Fred's behavior with the patterns of functional and electromagnetic images. The proper location to implant for recording of the impulses that would trigger the need for our therapy must be in those images you acquired from Fred's brain. It will take a very methodic and intelligent examination of the images and behavioral data to identify the targets in the brain for recording and stimulation. If you identify them, it will be much easier to reapply for the money if the response of the reviewers at this time is negative. Don't feel discouraged by Dr. Mallory's comments; he tends to be a little negative. It is part of the scientific skepticism that makes him a good scientist;" said Dr. Hillary.

"Kids, just work hard, use your brains and enjoy the ride. We will get funded at some point and you will finish your degrees and develop this therapy. I am sure we all will be very proud of ourselves at that time," completed Dr. Hillary.

"This meeting is already too long. I have a lot of work to do. See you all another time," said Dr. Larsson, standing up and walking to his desk in the main part of the laboratory. The others also left, laughing at his impatience.

Chapter 18
Pressure Builds Up

Jill was already 7 months into her pregnancy when she received the letter of acceptance to medical school and in the UCLA Medical Scientist Training Program, allowing her to do a doctorate in philosophy in parallel with her medical doctor studies. Charles and Jill were thrilled. She would start next September, three months later. She would be a mother taking care of a newborn by then. Charles and she were already preparing the home for the new baby. Charles would have little of his course work left, being mostly dedicated to his research. Although tight, the schedule they were planning seemed feasible. They knew that they would not have any extra time for the baby's or their own extra needs, such as a possible illness or the need to work for more money.

Randall was born on schedule. He was a boy who during the first month, took all available time from Jill. She was on vacation and fascinated by motherhood. Charles was also fascinated and helped Jill at night, sharing the feeding and sharing duties so she could get some sleep. They knew, from the discussions with Dr. Hillary, that they needed to learn to live on a few hours of sleep. This worried Jill. She knew she could function on very few hours of sleep, but her concern was that lack of sleep could make Charles very moody. Fortunately, she couldn't see any reason for anxiety or challenges due to Charles. He was working alone in the laboratory of nano-devices. Micro electrical circuits would keep him for hours in the laboratory looking at a microscope connecting micro wires. Charles was happy with his work and not being challenged by his advisor.

School started. Jill asked Charles to be at home with the baby while she went to classes. She would study at home as soon as she could leave school and let him go to the laboratory. Charles' advisor in the laboratory understood their pressing schedule and allowed Charles to organize his own working hours. The first semester went very well. The baby started to sleep all night long. Jill could study after dinner until late while Charles was in the laboratory. Jill started on vacation and organized her time so she could have mornings in the computer laboratory to analyze Fred's images. Charles would work on his project after lunch and until late at night while she stayed with the baby. During this period they managed baby, school and research in a very harmonic way. Jill's grades were outstanding, and Charles' first device was completed.

School started again and this semester, Jill's schedule became more demanding. She was committed to classes in mornings and afternoons; Charles was left with only nights to do his research. He slept in the afternoon while the baby was having his nap. He studied his own subjects during the day while watching the baby and cooked the meals for Jill. He even made a brown bag lunch for her to take to school. They were living an efficient student and parents' life. They were not having time for each other, however.

During the weekends, they divided their time studying and watching the baby. They did not have time for distractions. Too much work and no play; their relationship was becoming dull. They were not even sleeping together because most of the nights Charles spent in the laboratory. His advisor asked about his progress. The device he had built did not work well; moreover, it was too big. The advisor asked him to come to work during the day so he could help. Charles needed to discuss his project with other students and scientists working on similar projects. The advisor felt that, working alone, Charles would likely follow the wrong pathways. Charles explained the situation, but the advisor was adamant that he could not continue on with the night schedule. He was not receiving the proper support and education that a graduate student like him deserved and needed.

Charles left the laboratory, feeling annoyed, and approached Jill when he got home.

"Honey, we will have to change our schedule arrangement. My advisor wants me to come during the day to the laboratory. He usually leaves at 4PM; I have to be there while he is there for at least 3 hours. I need to overlap my time with his and other scientists in the laboratory. He feels strongly that we have to cross-pollinate our ideas to achieve better and faster results," said Charles.

"It makes sense, but it will be difficult, Charlie, my morning class finishes at 11AM and the afternoon class starts at 1 PM. I have only time for lunch."

"Could you leave a little early and come home for three hours during lunch time? I would arrive at the laboratory at 10 AM; you would lose the last hour of your morning class. At least you would have a good idea of what was studied, you could complete the study of the subject at home and gather the notes of one of your colleagues," suggested Charles.

"Well, I guess we will have to do that. Then I will return for the afternoon class at 1:00PM. It may work for a while. Hopefully at least until your advisor feels you are headed in the right direction in your project. We knew that we would have to sacrifice somewhere. As it is now, you have sacrificed more than your teacher can accept. Let's see how far I can push my teachers. Then we will come up with another idea. Unfortunately, we don't even have extra money for a babysitter. We could ask your mother or my mother to help, but it is only one hour per day, it is not worth it to bring them from San Diego only for this. They also work; they cannot be here one hour in the middle of the day," Jill said.

"At least if the NIH grant had been funded we would be in a better situation now, we probably would have a salary and could afford a babysitter," said Charles.

"Yes, but we would also have much more pressure to perform from Dr. Mallory's laboratory," said Jill. "I am sure that Dr. Hillary would manage Dr. Mallory, so he wouldn't put pressure on us. He apparently understands very well the pressure we are under now," said Jill.

"Yes, Dr. Hillary already told me he has been through what we are going through now. That is why he encouraged us to take this incredible amount of work," said Charles.

"Yes, he is of the opinion that busy people are the ones that get things done. What I think is that it's a hell of a lot of pressure. I don't know if I'm having the fun that Dr. Hillary made it out to be," said Jill.

"Come on, you always come home all excited about your physiology classes. When you are looking at the baby, you almost drool. You also spend hours looking at Fred's brain images trying to figure out patterns. Jill you love it all, it is just that you don't see it because we are getting so tired. I admire so much your dedication."

"Charlie, you are too much in love. I just don't know how spending so much time without relating closely to each other, we still maintain this incredible love. We must be crazy or very special people. I don't know about me, but you are very special," said Jill.

"I vote for you as the special one. I love you."

They settled into their new schedule. They barely had time to eat and certainly had no time to talk with each other. Each day they met at the door, when one entered the other immediately left. Randall was now one year old. Charlie had finished his course work and intensified his work in the laboratory. Jill started her second year of medical school; the grant application from the laboratory did not get funded for the second time and was now in the third revision. Jill and Charles were using their financial reserves. They had enough for 4 years from Charles' advertisement contracts at the time of the World Cup. At least if the grant was funded, they would have a salary and afford a baby sitter during the day. Life would turn into heaven again; they needed so much a break. Charles and Jill looked exhausted all the time.

Dr. Mallory was getting discouraged; Dr. Larsson had his job threatened for lack of funds for his salary. Dr. Hillary was supporting the laboratory with funds from grateful patients' donations and companies interested in the results of the laboratory. The price of primate research was becoming prohibitive with the university increases in the per diem for the animals. The whole group was under a lot of stress.

Charles was now sleeping three to four hours per day. Randall started to have periods of crying at night and for several hours during the day. Jill missed classes and took him to the pediatrician. He had a urinary infection. He was placed on antibiotics, but the crying did not improve for a whole week.

Charles came home one day to find Jill sleeping with her head over her books and Randall crying. He woke her up with a kiss.

"Dear, I have been waiting for you. I need to go to the library and finish up a search. I need some articles for tomorrow, I have a paper due," said Jill.

"Sorry dear, I didn't know. I had a lot of work in the laboratory; I had to stay late. I believe that the library is closed now, go to sleep, I will take care of Randall," he rushed to take the baby who didn't stop crying.

"I can't believe you didn't come earlier! I called the laboratory, nobody answered. I was so worried about you! I am very upset! I don't know what to do tomorrow. This paper is so important. I may flunk this class," said Jill.

"Did you give Randall his 6 PM dose of antibiotic?" ask Charles.

"No, what time is it?" asked Jill.

"I can't believe you didn't give him his medication! That is why he is crying! He also has a fever! Did you feed him? It is already 11 PM!" said Charles.

"I can't believe I slept so long. I decided to take a half-hour nap while waiting for you. I was so tired. You were supposed to be here at six. I was relying on you to wake me up and give him the medication while I would dash out the door to the library. I left a message on the laboratory phone, did anybody give it you?" asked Jill impatiently.

"When you are with the baby, it is your responsibility, you cannot rely on somebody picking up a message on an answering machine to take care of a sick child," said Charles.

"Look who is talking, you were the one that should have been here 5 hours ago!" Jill said.

"You are the one who slept 5 hours and didn't even care for your baby. In years, I haven't slept a complete 5 hours!" said Charles.

"For starters, he is our baby, not only my baby. You are too selfish with your work," said Jill.

Charles' expression changed; he walked in her direction with Randall in his arm. He almost threw the baby at her. He closed his fists and his eyes. Clearly, he was making an extreme effort to control himself. He walked backward in the direction of the door. He opened the door, turned, and started running. He left the building through the back door in the alley and started walking fast.

The alley was dark. He saw a car parked and two guys talking. He was walking by fast when one of them grabbed his arm. They were college students, young but strong. Charles jolted his arm, but the one was holding his other arm asked if he had any money and if he wanted to buy drugs. He answered that he was not interested, but the guys demanded money. The fellow who he had jolted his arm from came toward him ready to punch him while his buddy held Charles from behind.

Charles, using the guy holding him as the fulcrum, lifted both legs and kicked the attacking guy in the face. He was now charged with rage and completely out of control. He released himself from the guy that was holding him and punched him in the middle of his chest with such force that the guy collapsed to the ground. Charles jumped over him and punched his face against the pavement. He punched him so many times that enough time passed for the other fellow to recover from the kick in the face and attack him from behind, removing him from the top of the other guy.

Charles turned his rage against the attacker and punched him in the belly. He repeated the same succession of punches that he used to knock out Ryan in the parking lot the day that Roberto stopped him from strangling Chris. Now, however, Charles was alone. He continued punching the fellow until he himself was limp and tired. He started walking down the alley leaving the bodies of the two guys on the ground. He woke up from his trance as he saw the streetlights on the corner of the alley. When he arrived under the light, two other college kids saw him. One immediately called 911 on his cell phone. Charles was bathed in blood.

Chapter 19
Electrical Discharge

Randall was flushed with a high fever and limp in Jill's arms. She rushed to the room to give his medication. She placed him in his crib and run to her bathroom to fetch the medication. When she returned, he was having an epileptic fit. He convulsed for few seconds contracting all muscles of his body. She was terrified by the contortions that the contractions generated in Randall's face. They reminded her in many ways the expression that minutes earlier had terrified her on Charles' face. She took him from the crib as the last contractions abated while he was in her arms to leave Randall in a deep slumber.

Desperately, she rushed to the hospital, running the two blocks from her apartment building to the emergency room door. When she entered the emergency room, Randall was still in a deep sleep. A tall triage nurse immediately recognized her. Jill had volunteered in the emergency room before she entered medical school.

"Hi! What is up?" asked the nurse in a friendly way.

"Please help me, my baby…" started Jill anxiously.

"Calm down, girl, your baby has a good color, he is just sleeping; I will take care of him. Go and register in that window. Give me the baby. I'll hold him for you. What is his name?"

"Randy," said Jill, yielding her the baby.

The nurse took the baby in to the receiving ward while Jill registered Randy and signed the hospital emergency room papers. *Scary*, she thought, she just gave the hospital the permission to do any medical procedure if necessary. She was so confused and worried about Randall and Charles. As she relaxed knowing that the baby was in good hands, her mind started to create sceneries of troubles that Charles could get into. She moved from the registration to the ward where Randall was already waking up. The nurse had given him medication for fever and called the pediatrician. She had already secured a vein for hydration and seizure medication infusion.

When Jill saw the saline bag hanging and the fluid flowing into Randall's vein, she became teary. The nurse hugged her and explained that it was necessary because the baby could have another seizure if medication were not given to prevent it. She also explained that the baby needed hydration. There was more than 6 hours that Randy was without food or drink. Jill laid her head in the tall nurse's chest and broke down sobbing.

"It is ok, febrile seizure is common in Randy's age. He will be fine. He will need to take medication for a while, but it will not affect him. Children develop normally after a febrile seizure. The majority of the time they will never have another again and remain completely cured as they grow up. Everything will be alright," reassured the nurse.

"Thank you," gasped Jill between sobs, "how long do you think that we will be here? I need to find my husband."

"Probably you will be here the whole night, the pediatricians will come, then the pediatric neurologist. I am sure that they will order a scan of Randy's brain and assure that he has proper anticonvulsant levels in his blood to protect him from seizures before discharging him. Do you want to go find your husband? I am already overtime, my shift just finished at 11, but I can stay and care for your baby until you return," offered the nurse.

"Oh! No. I would never leave Randy. May I use a telephone? I want to call my mother to ask for help," said Jill.

"Sure, dial nine and get an outside line. I'll try to expedite the pediatrician. It will be difficult, however; they may be busy and Randy is not in danger now. They will take their sweet time," said the nurse.

At this moment, Jill recognized a doctor walking toward her. It was Greg, a junior neurosurgery resident that she met one day in the cafeteria while talking with Dr. Hillary.

"What's up?" asked Greg smiling. He was a handsome, tall, broad-shouldered, blond hair guy with blue eyes, and was very nice.

"Hi! You look familiar. Where did I meet you?" asked Jill.

"In the cafeteria with Dr. Hillary, you look frazzled, may I help you?" asked Greg.

"My baby had a seizure, I just brought him in. We are waiting for a pediatrician. I guess he will need a scan of his brain. The nurse said that it would take the whole night to get it done. I guess I have to wait," said Jill.

"Let me expedite things for you, you are one of us, I'll make sure you have special treatment," said Greg with his wide and sympathetic smile.

"Thanks, I need so much to get out of here, I am so worried about my husband, I don't know where he is, he is not answering the telephone at home nor his cellular," said Jill.

"Ok, help me. I will take your son directly to the scanner. I have a friend there; we will scan him in no time. Then I'll page the pediatrician and talk with him. Let's go!" commanded Greg.

Greg guided the stretcher to the corridor and moved in the direction of the scanner with Jill helping him. The nurse immediately stopped them.

"Hi, wise guys, where do you think you are going? I need to know what is going on. I am taking care of Randy."

"Hi gorgeous," answered Greg. "Judy, I am just helping my friend here. She is becoming a neurosurgeon soon; she deserves special treatment. She is one of Dr. Hillary's students."

Judy opened up a huge smile. She had an obvious crush on Greg. She said, "I just saw Dr. Hillary; he is in the hospital. Do you want me to page him?"

"Please," Jill uttered.

"Let's not waste time," said Greg, pushing the stretcher. "Dr. Hillary will want to see a scan of the baby's brain anyway."

Jill continued helping Greg with the stretcher and the nurse went to page Dr. Hillary.

They arrived in the scanner room to find a patient with multiple injuries on the table. There was blood everywhere. He was bleeding from a big gash in the forehead that was wrapped in a tight drape. There were lines running in several directions, blood and saline were being infused at the same time and the patient breathing was being maintained by an anesthesiologist pumping a floppy bag. The senior neurosurgery resident was there and immediately harassed Greg.

"What are you doing taking care of pediatric cases when we have to remove this guy's intracranial clot? I am taking him to the operating room immediately; take a look at his scan. I will need your help."

Greg looked at Jill and said, "Sorry, Jill, this guy will be brain-dead in minutes if we don't act immediately."

"What about Randy?" Jill asked.

"He is fine. We need to remove this patient from the scanner and send him to the operating room. When I arrive in the operating room, I will make sure that Dr. Hillary knows that you are here."

"I will clean the room and scan your baby right away," reassured the scanner technician.

"Yes, Jill. When Dr. Hillary arrives, he will have the scan ready," said Greg and left with the patient to the operating room.

Jill found herself alone in the corridor with Randy, she started sobbing again. Soon the technician returned and asked her to help him bringing Randy to the scanner room. When Dr. Hillary arrived in the scanner room, the first series of images were already displayed in the scanner computer screen. Jill was with tears in her eyes. Dr. Hillary reassured her that those images were normal; however, he wanted images after contrast material intravenous infusion.

"Jill, we need to see the images after dye infusion; we need to rule out tumor or infection," said Dr. Hillary.

"Dr. Hillary, Randy just had a urinary infection, he is on antibiotics. I missed the dose 6 hours ago, he had fever and a seizure," explained Jill anxiously.

"So, most likely, he had just a febrile seizure, Randy will be fine. Just relax, Jill, it will be ok," reassured Dr. Hillary while he started walking out of the room.

"No, Dr. Hillary, I cannot relax, I am also worried about Charlie. He had a strange attack of rage. I don't know where he is and he is not answering our home phone nor his mobile."

"Calm down, girl, he is probably walking to calm himself down, he will show up," said Dr. Hillary.

"Please help me find him, he is working so hard. He has not slept well for ages. He never treated me like he did hours ago. He was not normal when he ran out of the house," insisted Jill.

"Jill, let's call the police and ask them to locate him, now I will have to go to the operating room to help the residents with that poly trauma patient. I promise that I will be back as soon as I can," said Dr. Hillary while he left the scanner room.

Jill followed him and said, "When Charlie is in his trance, anything can happen. We don't like to leave him alone in these circumstances. I already called his mother and my mother to help."

"Great, Jill, now you concentrate on Randy. I will trigger the police search for Charlie from the operating room. The nurse there will help me."

"Thanks, Dr. Hillary," said Jill.

"I'll check Randy's scans obtained after the dye injection when I finish in the operating room. Then I will go the emergency room to see Randy again; he will need to stay in observation until tomorrow, pending the final results of the scan and blood tests," said Dr. Hillary while he entered the operating room block and disappeared in the corridor.

Jill rushed back to the scanner. Judy, the tall emergency room nurse was already pushing the stretcher out of the scanner room. They went to the observation room in the emergency area.

Chapter 20
Trance

Charles was found by the police wandering in the streets of Westwood. They immediately took him to the police station and placed him in jail. Charles couldn't remember his own name. He could not say his address. Actually he was not answering to any questions. He appeared extremely depressed; his face was without any expression. He was just dirty with blood, including his face; this was mostly from his victims, because he was not hurt. The policeman thought that he was not informing just to avoid saying things that would compromise him further, so he decided to let Charles sleep to deal with him the next morning.

He said, "If you don't identify yourself, I will have to keep you here for a long time. I see that you are not hurt."

Charles lay in the little bed in his cell and took a fetal position. He finally fell into a deep slumber.

The policeman shook his head and said to his companion, "We deal with him tomorrow."

Chapter 21
So Much Violence

The two students were found in the alley two hours later and taken to the emergency room at UCLA. Greg was immediately called to see them. The triage doctor at the emergency room saw that a neurosurgeon would be needed. One patient had both pupils dilated and the other had only the right pupil dilated. Greg, after examining them, shook his head and said, "So much violence out there, this must be connected to drugs. Probably a gang beat these fellows for money. This one with both pupils dilated appears to be way beyond help, however let's send him to the scanner immediately."

"You don't think it is too late for any action? He is obviously brain-dead. Let's put our efforts on the other one, there we have a chance," said the triage doctor.

"You know, these bilaterally dilated pupils can be only eye trauma and not a sign of brain death, he is still having some spontaneous breathing. Let's secure his airway and send him to the scanner. He is young; we don't know how long ago he was hit. Moreover, this was not a high speed car accident, he may make it," and having said that, Greg moved to the next patient.

"This one has a good chance, he is definitely breathing spontaneously, and he localizes the pain stimulus on the right side, nothing on the left. He is however very weak on the left side. He also needs a secured airway; he will have to be sedated though to tolerate a tube through his throat. Call anesthesia to help. Also, advise the operating room that we may be going in soon. Let's take him to the other scanner."

The nurses had already catheterized the patient's vein and checked vital signs. Blood pressure was stable. Anesthesia arrived, assisted ventilation was established, and they wheeled the patient toward the scanner. Greg followed this patient to the scanner and called the neurosurgery senior resident for help. He was overwhelmed; two severe patients with neurosurgical problem like these would require a lot of manpower. He also asked the emergency room nurse to advise Dr. Hillary of the arrival of the two head trauma patients.

Dr. Hillary yelled from the operating field, "You are kidding! What a busy night! I am almost finishing here; Greg had to leave me alone to close when you called him there. I didn't know that there were two patients. I will be at the scanners soon. Ask the senior resident Jeff to help Greg. Greg is too junior to handle these two cases alone."

When Dr. Hillary entered the first scanner, Jeff was already placing an intracranial monitor in the patient with both dilated pupils.

"Any surgery here?" asked Dr. Hillary.

"No, the scanner shows no major intracranial bleeding or contusions, the patient is with stable vital signs; he is not reacting to pain however, and has both pupils dilated. I don't understand well what is going on," said Jeff.

"Most likely he had a major hypoxia; many times, the patient has a prolonged respiratory arrest due to a prolonged concussion at the time of the head blow. Acute scans don't show signs of lack of oxygenation. Only observation will tell us. You have to monitor his intracranial pressure to detect a possible delayed intracranial bleeding. Also, you will need the pressure information to manage a possible brain swelling. Moreover, this guy may be on drugs from all we know, let's observe him closely. Send him to the intensive care unit (ICU). See you later; I will check what Greg is up to in the other scanner."

"Great, you arrived! I am slightly confused here; I don't see a major intracranial bleeding to explain this patient's right side paralyzed pupil. He is too weak on the left side for the amount of abnormality I see on the CT scan. Something weird is going on," said Greg.

"Let me see the pictures. Look Greg, there is this contusion in the right frontal lobe, there is already swelling surrounding it. This patient has been unconscious for several hours for us to detect swelling already. This also explains why the other patient that was with him in the aisle looks so brain-dead. They both may be comatose for at least two hours," said Dr. Hillary.

"I was planning to place an intracranial monitor and send him the ICU for observation and treatment of the swelling, what do you think, Dr. Hillary?"

"No, he has a little bit of shift from right to left, see?" Dr. Hillary pointed the scanner screen.

"Yes, so what do we do?" asked Greg.

"We take him to the operating room now to remove the contusion. The contusion represents only already destroyed brain that will stay there just to release toxins from the death cells, causing irritation and swelling. This will obviously compromise his recovery, or even threaten his life. Let's remove it right away," said Dr. Hillary.

"Great, let's do it, Dr. Hillary, would you please see Jill in the emergency, she is anxious to talk with you about the contrasted scans. Her son is doing well."

"Thanks for reminding me, I was ready to start to work with you again. Greg, please take the patient to the operating room. Plan the classic large interrogation mark incision on his right frontal region, I will see the scans, discuss with Jill and then join you in the operating room. Have you removed one of these contusions before?"

"No, you have to come back soon, I need lots of help."

"Please page me when you have the patient positioned and prepped. Did they find Jill's husband?" asked Dr. Hillary.

"Not yet, she is very anxious."

"I will calm her down. See you in the OR soon, Greg."

Chapter 22
Hamartoma

It was now 4 o'clock in the morning; Jill was tired and fighting to stay awake. Randy was completely awake, but agitated. The nurse had her hands full; Randy would not stop trying to remove his IV catheter.

"I'm sorry, he is giving you such a hard time," said Jill to the nurse.

"No problem, this is my job."

"You need some rest, what time does your shift finish?"

"I am on the 11 PM to 7 AM shift. I am OK, you need some sleep," said the nurse.

"My mother and my mother-in-law must be arriving at any moment; I called them about 2 AM, after Randy's scan. I am so worried about my husband; did you hear anything about his search?" asked Jill.

"No, everybody got so busy with the two fellows that arrived about 15 minutes ago that nobody is talking about anything else but taking these guys to the operating room."

"Do you think they will be OK?" asked Jill, disinterested.

"I don't know, I didn't have time to see them, Randy has taken all my time."

"Go and have a break, drink some coffee and ask the front desk if they heard anything about my husband, Charles never disappears like this," said Jill.

"I'll take your offer; Randy is fine, just make sure that he does not remove his IV," said the nurse while she left the room.

Jill climbed in the large emergency room bed, lay on her side and placed Randy's head between her chest and her arm. She kissed his forehead. Immediately he calmed down. Soon he was asleep. She also slept. Ten minutes later, the nurse checked on them; when she saw that both were asleep, she smiled and took advantage of the break.

Dr. Hillary came to talk to Jill; when he saw that scene, he also smiled and took advantage to have a cup of coffee, before running to the operating room to help Greg. He met the nurse in the coffee break area and asked about Randy, "How is the boy doing?"

"He is agitated but fine now; he and Mom are asleep. I decided to let them rest a little. His labs came, all normal. His anticonvulsant level is also fine. Are you sending him home?" asked the nurse.

"No, I will keep him for the day, I need to take advantage and order an MRI, it will be easier to get the insurance to pay if we have it while he is here. I have a suspicion that he has a small hypothalamic hamartoma. The quality of the CT scan that he had, even with the contrast, was poor to see small details. It is good for ruling out bleeding, a major tumor or a vascular malformation, but not for a less than 5 mm hamartoma in the hypothalamus. We didn't order his hormonal panel, did we?" asked Dr. Hillary.

"No, there was no reason to order. We were all suspecting of a common febrile seizure. What is a hypothalamic hamartoma anyway?" asked the nurse.

"It is a neural tissue malformation that when in the hypothalamus can cause a variety of symptoms, mostly seizures of different kind, like crises of laughing, crises of aggression and even generalized seizures…" At this moment, his beeper rang.

"Sorry, I got to go to the OR, Greg is ready to start, I will explain to you latter, please don't mentioned anything to Jill, she would become more anxious. I will talk with her when I leave the OR. Bye!"

The nurse walked to the front desk and asked about the Charles search.

"Nothing, actually I called the police about 30 minutes ago, they didn't know anything. They promised to call me back if they find him," answered the clerk.

"Thanks, please let me know," said the nurse and walked to Randy's room. Jill and Randy were still asleep. She smiled again and sat in the chair close by to observe them and take her deserved rest.

Chapter 23
Hanging

At the change of shift in the police station, one of the on-call men told the arriving officers about Charles. He described this tall guy with a familiar face, but completely unresponsive. He probably remembered Charles' physiognomy from the days that he was a famous soccer player.

"We found him wandering, had an expressionless face, vague eyes, and blood in his hands, face and clothes. He clearly got into a fight. We collected his clothes for blood analyses and gave him a prisoner's pants and shirt. He fell asleep as soon as he entered the cell. He probably will wake up hungry and start talking. I haven't checked him this morning; it was busy here last night. Bye, have a good day."

When the arriving policeman went to the back room to check the prisoners, Charles was stretched on the floor. He had tried to hang himself from the bars of the jail door with the pants that they had given him. He had tied one leg around his neck, climbed the door mid-transverse bar and tied the other leg of the pants to the door upper transverse bar. Then he let his body fall backward. The pants split open in the middle; however, it must have held him hanging for a long enough time to make him unconscious. He was breathing heavily. Despite all efforts of the officer to wake him up, he remained comatose.

"Son of a gun!" screamed the police man. "Call the ambulance, this guy may die here."

The police station clerk called the ambulance and they took Charles immediately to the UCLA emergency room.

Chapter 24
Emergency Commotion

Jill woke up with a lot of commotion in the emergency room corridor close to her room. She saw that Randy was still asleep; he had good color and his respiration was calm and rhythmic. She stepped out of the bed and put her head out of the door to see what was going on and to ask for the nurse. Her nurse had already gone home; the tall nurse, Judy, had returned to her 7 to 7 shift and greeted Jill.

"Good morning, so you are still here. Looks like you had a rough night. How do you feel?"

"Fine, I slept about two hours. Have you seen Dr. Hillary?" asked Jill.

"No, he is still in the operating room with one of the two patients that arrived in the middle of the night. Apparently, the guy had several skull fractures."

"Have you heard when I'll take Randy home?"

"The other shift nurse told me that Dr. Hillary decided to admit Randy because he wants to see an MRI of his brain before you go home. He came here last night but you were asleep."

"Sorry I missed him, now I am more concerned with Charlie. I am relaxed about Randy; Dr. Hillary told me that Randy is fine. The CT scan without contrast was normal and the blood tests also came normal; I don't understand why we need to stay here," said Jill.

While they were talking, a stretcher was wheeled by them. Jill immediately recognized the man lying down. She screamed, "This is Charlie, what happened to him?"

"We don't know yet, we will take him to the receiving room to secure his airway. He came in an ambulance from a police station," said the triage nurse.

Jill started crying uncontrollably. Judy took her to the room, hugged her and comforted her.

"I will find out what is going on and let you know. Now I will transfer Randy to the pediatric ward," said Judy.

"Did you see my mother? She was supposed to be here by now, I need her to stay with Randy while I care for Charlie," said Jill.

"They arrived about half an hour ago, they checked you and Randy out and went to your apartment to leave their luggage and pick up Randy's things. They were planning to return in about one hour to send you home for some rest. They are also very tired; they drove in the middle of the night from San Diego. When they saw that you and Randy were resting, they decided to take care of few things before sending you home. They were also anxious about Charlie. They were expecting to find him in your home. I will call them, as soon as I have more information about Charles. Now you stay quiet here watching Randy while I will gather some information," said Judy.

"How can I be quiet here when Charlie might be dying in the next room? I'll go there for a minute," said Jill.

"No, you will not, they need to save his life right now, you will only disturb in the emotional state you are in at this moment. The best you can do is stay in your room and wait," said Judy, pushing Jill into Randy's room.

At this moment, Dr. Hillary walked in the corridor, still in his surgeon's clothes and asked Judy, "What is going on here?"

"Enter in the receiving room for you to check it out. Apparently, Jill's husband is there," said Judy.

"What happened?" He asked, entering the receiving area.

"Apparently, this guy tried to hang himself in the police station. He failed the suicide attempt, but is unconscious," answered the emergency room doctor.

"So, don't move his neck, he may have a hangman's fracture. We need a CT scan immediately to confirm that his neck is stable. Let's do a tracheotomy so he can breathe safely and let's take him to the scanner," said Dr. Hillary, starting to help his colleague.

Charles had recovered his color; the oxygen saturation was above 95% and his vital signs were fine. He was moving all extremities when stimulated with pain, actually he localized the site of the painful stimulus. Dr. Hillary sighed with relief. They took him to the CT scan after immobilizing his neck.

Chapter 25
Slit Neck

Jill gasped, crying, when Charles was wheeled by Dr. Hillary out of the receiving area in the stretcher. The strange procession moved in the corridor toward the scanner. Charles had his neck cut down with a tube coming out of the wound; he was wearing a strange looking orange shirt and being ventilated by the anesthesiologist following the stretcher. Dr. Hillary and Judy were guiding the stretcher walking fast. Charlie had blood throughout his face and was expressionless. Dr. Hillary was extremely serious, unusual for him, as he was always trying to make situations light. Jill had never seen that worried expression in Dr. Hillary's face. She immediately understood that the situation was serious.

At this moment, Jill's and Charles' mothers entered the corridor and saw the desperation in Jill's face. Her mother ran to her and embraced her, while Charles' mother ran to the stretcher and started crying. Soon the stretcher cleared the corridor and disappeared behind the emergency room swinging doors into the guts of the hospital, entering the radiology department. Jill returned to Randy's room, sat on the chair, and sobbed.

"Oh Mother! This is too much; please tell me that everything will be alright."

"Sometimes, Jill, all seems unbearable, but inside of yourself you have the strength to handle any situation; you know that I will be at your side. I will not leave you alone at this moment," said her mother, hugging her.

"Jill, I will take you home," said Charles' mother. "Your mother will stay here with Randy, you need some serious rest; you have been through so much. Let's go."

"OK," said Jill.

Jill was exhausted, she couldn't think. She was in shock with Charles' appearance. She wanted to cry, but she couldn't. She looked down and let her mother-in-law guide her out of the emergency room.

Judy returned from the scanner and asked Jill's mother to help her to take Randy to the pediatric ward. She explained to her that Dr. Hillary wanted Randy to stay overnight for an MRI scan and that all seemed fine with Randy. She also explained that Charles was in the scanner and would most likely need a surgery in his neck to stabilize his fracture. Dr. Hillary was already preparing the operating room for him.

Chapter 26
Result of the Violence

Jill could not sleep. She was beyond feeling tired. She was stressed out and anxious to talk to Dr. Hillary. All had happened so fast. She assumed that Randy's illness was under control; however Charles was almost losing his life, or his ability to move because of his dangerous cervical spine fracture. Beside herself, Jill walked the streets of Westwood guided by Charles' mother toward her home. Both women were in such state of shock that they would not look or talk to each other. They were seeing the result of Charles' lack of self-control, a state that they fought against throughout their lives.

They still did not know, however, that the two young men that arrived before Charles were linked to the tragedy they were living. Soon they would come to the realization that it was not only Charles' health that they had to fight for, but also for his freedom.

The first young man arriving with completely dilated pupil was declared brain-dead few hours after arriving in the intensive care unit. He showed no signs of life, except for his young heart that kept maintaining his body functions. The rhythm of his heartbeat was amazingly constant, with a perfect recording in the monotonous beeping monitor of his vital signs. His blood pressure was maintained normal with medication and his intracranial pressure had skyrocketed out of control. It was way higher than his arterial blood pressure, a sign that blood was no longer flowing through his brain. The electrical recording of his brain waves was showing flat lines. The doctor responsible for the intensive care unit had already contacted the family asking for donation of his organs for transplantation. Such young and healthy organs could be used to save lives of people waiting in the long waiting lists of renal, heart and liver transplants. Heart breaking as it sounds; the conversation with his family went well. The family wanted to donate the organs. They were shocked with the news of their son's murder. They were making a financial sacrifice to send him to study in Los Angeles. They were told that he was assaulted and killed in one of the Westwood streets for money. These were good people from the desert in California wanting to be helpful to humanity. They had no idea that their son was involved in the traffic of drugs.

The other young man was still in the intensive care unit; however, his intracranial pressure was under control, and he was starting to move all his extremities. He was still depending on the ventilator and on medication to maintain his arterial blood pressure at high levels. It was important to maintain the perfusion of blood through his recovering brain. Better milieu for his brain recovery would dictate how useful his life would be in the future. Would he be able to continue his studies, or even work in the future? His fate was unknown, but most likely he would survive with severe brain damage and depend on an institution or his family for the rest of his life. His family was not as settled as the first young man, they wanted all done to save his life and to find out who had assaulted their son. They knew of their son's involvement in drugs, but they wanted that the person causing so much damage to him to be punished. Charles would have to answer to the law, a process that Jill or his mother had no idea that they would have to face.

It was already afternoon when Dr. Hillary left the operating room after 5 hours of surgery fixating Charles high cervical vertebrae. A complex construct of wires and screws was fashioned to maintain his neck stable and avoid damage of his spinal cord. Charles was saved from possible paralysis; his brain, however, was still suppressed with high doses of barbiturates used during the anesthesia and to protect it from possible lack of oxygen. He was maintained on artificial breathing through the tube passing the cut down in his neck and lodged into his trachea. The constant rhythm of the ventilator kept his life while the ICU monitors showed excellent brain waves, heartbeat and normal blood pressure. Although in a guarded state, Charles was on the way to recovery, most likely a full recovery.

Dr. Hillary was exhausted and ready to go home. He went directly from the operating room to the emergency room to find out that Jill had gone home and was sleeping since midmorning. He also learned that Randy was awake and playing with his grandmother in the pediatric ward. The MRI of his brain had been completed and the proton density sequence showed a small abnormality. He saw the films, discharged Randy to go home and went to his own home for some rest. He advised Greg to page him in case of any Charles' or the young man's deterioration. Greg was also exhausted. He went home and passed the orders to his colleague resident coming to cover the call.

Chapter 27
Lots of Blood

Jill woke up with Randy, arriving home late that evening. He was on antibiotics and anticonvulsants, a medication to prevent seizures. She asked her mother and her mother-in-law to stay with Randy and rushed to the hospital to check on Charles. Arriving in the intensive care unit, she found Dr. Hillary already back from his short rest; he was called to care for Charles. Charles had woken up agitated and pulled out his endotracheal tube from his neck. He started bleeding through the cut down in his neck and with his coughing to expel the blood entering into his lungs; blood was sprinkled throughout his bed and all the way to the ceiling of the ICU.

The scenery was so shocking that the resident on call became desperate, having to call Dr. Hillary back from his deserved rest. The nurse in the unit did not allow Jill to enter until the situation was under control, preventing her from seeing such an alarming situation. After Dr. Hillary had sedated Charles, controlled the bleeding, and the nurse had cleaned the spilled blood, Jill was allowed in. Dr. Hillary was actually in good spirits.

"Jill, Charles is coming along great. He already showed purposeful movements and is breathing spontaneously. I feel that tomorrow I will allow him to be completely awake in an attempt to remove his breathing tube and send him to the ward."

"I heard while I was waiting that all in here was a mess with blood everywhere because Charles pulled out the tube in his neck. Do you think that he will behave enough to be out of here in such a short period?" asked Jill anxiously.

"I believe he is out of danger regarding his life. His neck fracture is stable, and his brain is working properly, at least to defend himself from a very bothersome tube entering his trachea. This endotracheal tube is very irritating, patients do try pulling it out when they wake up," answered Dr. Hillary.

"Between my mother, his mother and I, we will be with him all the time, being sure that he does not hurt himself," said Jill.

"No worry, the ward has a step-down unit with full-time supervision. We will start with him there. Then, maybe you, your mother and his mother can stay with him. I just do not know how his emotional state will be when he comes out of this sedation. He may be very aggressive, or very depressed. From his actions today, I assume he will be very aggressive. I may have to call the psychiatric people to help us."

"This is what scares me. His mood has been so unpredictable. He is under too much pressure. We have been so busy; we have been living in constant lack of sleep and lack of attention to each other. School has been so demanding for him and me. I am starting to get desperate."

"Girl, you need some pep talk. I take it you got some sleep since this morning. It was wise. You have a lot to digest from all that happened. Let's go to the cafeteria for a coffee and some time together."

They found a table in a quiet area of the cafeteria to avoid being interrupted. Dr. Hillary started the conversation carefully.

"Jill, the situation is very complicated. I believe that the days ahead of you will bring you so much understanding of the medical profession that will be worth years of training. You will have the opportunity to live the other side of the medical life. Few doctors have this opportunity. Consequently, many take medical decisions lightly. For example, when we discuss with a patient and his family about having a surgery, we tend to minimize the risks. Not only to decrease their anxiety, but also to convince them to accept the needed operation. Sometimes we become even insensitive to their worries and questions. This happens when we are under a lot of pressure in a busy day of duty in the hospital. Sometimes families complain to me that residents brush them off when they ask questions."

"Dr. Hillary, I know you like to teach, but please cut to the chase. What is going on that you feel I need to know and that is being so difficult for you to tell me?"

"A lot has happened, a lot I have to tell you, a lot I have difficulty to tell you, but I believe you can handle all. I just want to minimize things for you. Let's deal first with Charles' issues; I believe that Randy's problems we should handle in a near future when you bring him to my office for a consultation. I need to check his anticonvulsants levels and refer him to a pediatric neurologist to follow him for a while. We will talk about this later."

"Thank you, Dr. Hillary, I understand that the pressing issue at this moment is Charles. You told me that you believe that his life is out of danger, what is worrying you? Is there anything else besides the well-known aggressive and depressive outbursts that cluttered his life for so many years?"

"Yes, Jill. The police have identified Charles as the attacker of the two guys that arrived before him in the emergency room. One of the fellows was declared brain-dead and is out for organ donation. Therefore, his attack is considered a murder."

"How do they know that he was the attacker?"

"The blood on his clothes matched the blood of the brain-dead patient, and moreover, they also found the blood of the second patient on his clothes," explained Dr. Hillary.

"But this does not prove that Charles was the attacker, it could be that someone just tried to incriminate him!" Jill uttered.

"Yes, but they also found Charles' blood on the fellows' clothes. Charles hurt his hands during the fight. I believe that they have a criminal case against Charles. Charles will have to respond to this at some point."

"This is awful, Dr. Hillary! We fought against this all our lives. He has already a police file. It will just hurt him further."

"Jill, there are always ways out. Charlie has been an outstanding sportsman, student, and husband. We know that this was in self-defense. We will be able to construct a case to keep him out of prison. We need, however, to find a way to control his reactions once and for all. This current admission to the hospital may be our opportunity. Let's use our brains."

Dr. Hillary was called to the ICU.

Chapter 28
End of the Line

There was lots of blood again, everywhere in the ICU. All happening around Charles' bed and ceiling. Charles was surrounded by nurses and residents trying to contain him. He was fighting everyone. He had hands and legs tied to the bed, and they were still holding him to no avail. Immediately Dr. Hillary ordered an intravenous injection of propofol, putting Charles asleep in few seconds. Dr. Hillary also understood then that it was time to take the endotracheal tube out of his neck. The tracheotomy had to be closed; it was only a source of irritation for Charles as he was no longer at risk of losing his airway. He was already becoming too awake to tolerate a tube in his trachea. This could be the source of all of Charles' fighting   Dr. Hillary asked the nurses to call the anesthesiologists to put a breathing tube through Charles' mouth, planning to close the incision in his neck. The next day, he would allow Charles to be completely awake and remove the tube from his mouth. He would be able to breathe on his own and then be transferred to the ward. It was done.

The problem was that even without the tube in his throat, Charles continued to be extremely agitated. He would become aggressive and uncontrollable always when he came out of heavy sedation. He needed incredible amounts of medication to stay in bed. He had to be asleep without interaction with people. This was necessary for the fracture in his neck to heal enough to keep his cervical spine stable. Jill was getting frustrated because she could not communicate with him. He was actually not participating as a living creature; he was only sleeping.

After several weeks of this heavy sedation, Charles was transferred to the psychiatric ward. At this time, his neck was already healed, both from the endotracheal tube incision and from the cervical fracture fixation. Enough new bone had been formed around his cervical fracture that he would not be able to destroy his cervical fixation metal construct and hurt himself. Now it was time to try to wake Charles and control him with oral medication. The psychiatrists were the ones with the knowledge to accomplish this next stage of Charles' recovery.

Charles continued, however, to be uncontrollable. He was either completely sedated with very little interaction with the ones around him or too aggressive to be physically unrestrained. To maintain him physically contained was impossible, impractical, and inhumane. Charles was a very strong fellow; nothing would contain him without hurting him. Soft music and soft movies had no effect on him. His mother tried all she learned over the years that would bring him to senses; Jill also spent hours and days with him trying to bring out of him his peaceful being. Nothing was working. Dr. Hillary finally called Jill aside for a conversation.

"Jill, we have to do something more drastic. I thought so much about Charles situation that I don't see any way out, but surgery. I just don't know for sure the best approach to help Charles. I need your help and dedication to decide what to do. I need more information on Charles' brain function. Do you think you can help me?"

"Sure, but please be more specific, I have no idea how I can help. I have done everything I know," answered Jill.

"Jill, you know more than you think you know, that is why I have so much hope that you can help Charles in a major way. You are a very wise person, Jill. You have acquired a very important skill when you observed Fred's rage attacks. You identified when it would start based on his pupillary dilation. You found the very moment to inject isotopes to study Fred's brain. I need you to use this skill to identify when Charles will become aggressive. I have a plan in mind. It will take a lot of work from you, me and our team, but I believe that we can come up with the proper surgery for Charles. It can be a breakthrough to help other people needing the same help. We have an opportunity to disclose the site in the brain needing intervention at the moment of rage onset, we may be able to control Charles' savage impulses and still maintain his incredible intelligence, sensitivity, and drive."

"Please, explain how we will proceed to identify this site in Charles' brain," said Jill anxiously.

"I believe that if we manage to obtain PET scans of Charles' brain at the time of rage onset and compare the images with his brain under sedation, we may be able to identify the specific area needing intervention. The idea is identical to the experiments that we performed with Fred. It would be extremely important that you scrutinize Fred's data in comparison to the data that we will obtain from Charles. If they match, it will be double confirmation of a fact. It will be enough for me to bring him to surgery. This is mainly because I am not planning to perform a destructive surgery in his brain. We have already technology good enough to make the surgery reversible and to give Charles control of his aggressive behavior. He will have to volitionally turn the device on for it to work; this leaves room for possible failure. It is far from the ideal, but still a hopeful solution."

"Dr. Hillary, let's do it, count on my complete commitment. I hate seeing Charles in this state. I miss so much my old Charlie; I am sure that his mother feels the same and will agree with your surgery proposal."

"Jill, we will need to call a meeting with Dr. Larsson, Dr. Mallory, and Dr. Bernard. Dr. Bernard's opinion and acceptance of our surgical suggestions is of utmost importance. As a psychiatrist, he will have to agree with our plans. Without his agreement we cannot proceed with surgery, even if you and Charles' parents beg for it. I will take care of the details."

Chapter 29
Board of Scientists

The team met again on a Saturday morning. Saturdays were the only days that all could take from their busy schedule do have a creative and productive meeting. During the week all had their time committed to surgeries, experiments, classes, administrative duties and academic trips. It was virtually impossible to organize a meeting in the schedule of these busy people. The relief of Charles and his family suffering became, however, priority for the team.

Even Dr. Bernard was touched by the situation. He had not seen a case so resistant to medical therapy. He had even thought of a trial of Electric Convulsive Therapy (ECT) to change the course of Charles' disease, however he felt it to be a too drastic measure and without firm scientific or clinical support. ECT was still used for severe refractory depression, but not for uncontrollable aggressive behavior. Dr. Bernard was actually excited with the possibility of a novel therapy for difficult cases. Drugs carried frequent undesirable side-effects that made the compliance with therapy difficult for such patients.

Dr. Hillary opened the meeting by reviewing Charles' medical history and all therapies offered to him over the years and during this current admission to the hospital. The first question came from Jill.

"Why do you think that Charles is not responding to the medications which were effective for him over the years?"

Dr. Bernard, as the typical psychiatrist, took control of the conversation, starting to digress on resistance to medication that can develop over periods of long-term use. He also discussed at length the lack of compliance of patients with similar disease. His explanations were heard attentively by all because the group was interested on learning all it could to formulate an intelligent strategy at the end of the meeting.

"Dr. Bernard, how frequently you see patients out of control like Charles?" asked Dr. Larsson.

"I don't remember of a case as difficult as Charles' case. I believe that patients as severe as Charles end up in prison early on, way before they make to the hospital. I believe Charles is still a free man because of his supportive and protective family."

Dr. Hillary interrupted to bring the discussion into focus with his opinion and his answer to Jill's very pertinent question.

"I believe that the hypoxia that Charles' brain was subjected to after he tried to hang himself, had a profound and lasting effect on his brain. I am starting to believe that he has lost important circuitry in his brain that gave partial control to his aggressiveness in the past. Although, the explanations that Dr. Bernard gave us are plausible for patients in long-term use of medication, Charles never used medication for long periods. Medications made him too dull for him to accept them. Even his family was averse to him using medication for too long."

"Do you have a suggestion of which circuitry was damaged in his brain?" asked Dr. Mallory skeptically.

"I wish I knew," answered Dr. Hillary, "but I have a hunch that it is in a similar site to the one we liberated in Fred's brain when we deprived him of his alcohol daily dose. I have asked Jill to scrutinize that data further, the site for intervention must be in those images we obtained at the moment of Fred's rage outburst onset."

"I have looked at that data so many times with Jill. I don't know how we can extract more information from those experiments and even if we do, I don't believe it to be enough information to infer an operation in the human brain," advanced Dr. Larsson doubtfully.

"We acquired new and powerful software in our radiation and functional surgery section. We can magnify images analyzing them to the level of pixels and voxels. Findings on images can now be related to electrical effects in the brain in a quantifiable way. I strongly believe that it is time to revisit Fred's data with this new software. Moreover, I intend to obtain similar data from Charles' brain," said Dr. Hillary excitedly.

"You are not telling us that we will repeat Fred's experiments using Charles, are you?" asked Larsson shaking his head.

"Precisely," answered Dr. Hillary. "I intend to ask Jill to use her acquired skills to obtain similar data. Obviously, it will be much easier. We don't need to go through all the conditioning and catheterization we did for Fred with Charles, that was what took too much of our time. All the catheterization is already done, only an intra-arterial line need to be added. This is a very simple procedure for our anesthesiologists and residents."

"The main work will be for Jill to observe all Charles' reactions at the very moment he is becoming aggressive. Because he is so heavily medicated, I would like to take him off the oral and control him with intravenous medication. Then we will be in position to observe him when he is getting out of the sedation and starting his aggressive behavior. The signs should be well determined and reproducible, so we can use them to time the injection of radioactive epinephrine and serotonin as we did for Fred. PET scans will be obtained with the drugs injected in the sedated state and at the time of the rage onset."

"Images will be compared, and differences may be detected. We will compare these differences with the ones observed in Fred's brain. The plethora of knowledge obtained from this exercise may be enough for me to adventure the implant of an electrical stimulating device in the site identified as crucial for the rage onset."

"I believe that I already know the signs; I cannot forget his face and eyes at the moment he backed off from me and Randy in our home and rushed into the alley. He was able to control himself at that moment. It was just before a full display of one of his rage episodes," interrupted Jill.

Dr. Hillary continued, "Great, Jill, if we work expeditiously, I believe we will be in position to perform these studies in approximately two weeks. The preparation for the experiments will be in parallel to the discontinuation of Charles' oral medication and transition to intravenous infusion. What do you think, Dr. Bernard?"

"Feasible, the yield is obviously unknown and unlikely. I am interested, however, on trying anything for Charles; I am getting frustrated with his lack of response to all my efforts. I am out of ammunition and ready to commit to your suggestions. Are radioactive tagged epinephrine and serotonin readily available?"

"Not readily, but it is possible to prepare them in our laboratory. These drugs are not used in routine imaging of the brain; however, with proper permission of the hospital research committee we can produce them. The isotope is short lived; we need to time the experiment perfectly like we did for Fred," advanced Dr. Larsson.

"We will do all the supportive work to obtain the images in our research scanner; our resolution is way better than that of the clinical scanner. Again, we will have to obtain all the permissions from the HSPC for the radioactive tagged drugs and use of the research scanner. We also have to convince the other scientists using the scanner that we need special time in the machine. It is difficult to obtain free time in the scanner for projects that are not planned a long time in advance."

"Usually, the basic science scientists have no understanding and are very skeptical of any clinical research project. They feel that very little yield is obtained from studies in humans. The data is usually very variable and poorly controlled. I will have to meet with the chief of the department to obtain permission. I will let you know when we can use the scanner. We should count with some negative answers before we can convince our colleagues of the importance of these studies," said Dr. Mallory.

"I believe we will find plenty of roadblocks, but we need to set tasks and deadlines to each one of us, if we want to accomplish this in two weeks. I would suggest that I deal with the HSPC, Dr. Mallory deals with the scanner time, Dr. Larsson arranges for the preparation of the tagged drugs, Dr. Bernard will decrease progressively Charles' medication and Jill will observe Charles' changes with the decrease of the medication. Jill you need to keep a log of every change observed when Dr. Bernard decreases the medication dose. Dr. Bernard can orient you. Additionally, I will ask you to transfer all Fred's scans data to our new computers. We will need to do the data transfer to compare Fred's and Charles' PET scans. We will need a very high level of magnification of Fred's and Charles' scans if we hope to discover our site of action in Charles' brain," finished Dr. Hillary.

"I believe that in less than one week, we will have to transfer Charles to a more controlled bed than the psychiatric ward. What do you suggest, Dr. Hillary?" asked Dr. Bernard.

"Just let me know when you need the transfer, I will arrange the bed in the neurosurgery ward and ICU as soon as you need," answered Dr. Hillary and the meeting was adjourned.

Chapter 30
Blander

Jill was in the cafeteria having breakfast after a long night observing Charles, when Greg came along.

"Hi Jill, how is Randy?"

"He is fine; he went home three weeks ago. Nothing important I believe, just a febrile seizure."

"Have you talked to Dr. Hillary about his scans? I believe they found a hamartoma in his hypothalamus."

"What are you talking about, Greg? I don't know of any abnormality in Randy's scans," said Jill, obviously very alarmed.

"Sorry to break this news to you so suddenly, I thought that Dr. Hillary had told you."

"No he didn't, and I just don't need one more problem to handle. I don't believe that Dr. Hillary didn't prepare me for this." She stood up and walked away, very upset.

Greg followed her, but she rushed into the elevator when the door was closing. He lost her. Without knowing what to do, Greg paged Dr. Hillary to tell him of his mistake. He felt very awkward. He already cared so much for Jill, admired her and actually hadn't been able to take her off his thoughts since that night in the emergency room. He had a keen desire to help her and protect her. He did not understand well his feelings for Jill. He believed he just wanted to comfort her in her difficulties. He felt deeply sorry for her. Dr. Hillary was in surgery, answering only 5 hours later.

Greg asked immediately, "Have you talked with Jill about Randy's scans?"

"No Greg, I didn't have the time or the courage to talk with her while she is going through so many problems with her husband."

"So I made a big mistake. I just broke the news to her. She ran away without giving me the chance to explain anything."

"Well, I will talk about your mistake later, now please help me to find her. She must be in a terrible state. Randy is actually in San Diego with her parents. She is too busy with Charles in the psychiatric ward to care for him." "She is either in the computer laboratory or with Charles. I will go to the ward, and you go to the computer laboratory. If you find her, please bring her to the cafeteria, we will meet there in 15 minutes. Bye."

They convened there 15 minutes later. Jill was nowhere to be found.

"Let's have a coffee, Greg, we need to talk."

"Sure, I am so sorry for all this, the least I wanted is cause more problems for poor Jill. I had no idea that you hadn't told her of the hamartoma."

"Sometimes Greg, we doctors are better with our mouths shut. Mainly when there is no appropriate therapy at the moment and the patient's relatives are not prepared to receive the news. It behooves us to prepare them for the information. Many times we need to dose what we say; mostly advancing solutions before the final news to give them hope and the understanding that together we will find a way out. Even if the way out is limited to minimizing suffering. The information has to be completely given, but in a progressive and rational way. Doctors learn to deliver difficult news over years of work and experiences like the one you just had. Some will never learn, maybe because although intelligent, they don't have sensitivity to care enough for the patient's relatives."

"Sorry I was so insensitive; I hope you are not upset with me."

"I don't need to be upset with you, Greg. The fact you are sorry and understood the mistake is enough. You will beat yourself about this long enough for you to remember next time you need to talk with a patient or their relatives about a severe disease and guarded prognosis. Now I need you to find Jill. I have a lot of things to do before I can look for her. If you see her, please call me immediately, I will have to spend some time calming and explaining to her my plans for Randy."

"I am on call today. I will have very little time myself, but I will do my best to look around the hospital for her. Did you call her home?"

"No, could you please do so? Bye."

Chapter 31
Hospital Security

Dr. Hillary was going to the recovery room to check on the patient he had just finished operating on when he was paged overhead to the psychiatric ward. He was divided where to go first because he was very anxious to see the patient in the recovery room. He had removed a benign tumor from the patient's area of the brain controlling the right side of the body and very close to the patient's speech center. Because the patient bled profusely during the tumor resection, some uncertain blood vessel coagulation was necessary. This made him very worried with the final outcome of the patient's right side and speech function.

A CT scan was ordered to assure the bleeding had indeed stopped and a post-operative clot was not forming in the tumor resection cavity. If there was a clot or active bleeding and the patient's right side was paralyzed, he had to intervene promptly to avoid permanent damage of this very functional area of the patient's brain. He decided to go see the patient first, assuming that the call from the psychiatric ward was from Greg reporting on Jill's whereabouts and Charles' state.

The overhead paging system called his name again, at this time asking him to go to the psychiatric ward at once. There was an emergency occurring there. Although divided, he rushed to the psychiatric ward. The paging system continued calling attention to the psychiatric ward, now with the security of the hospital also being called there. Dr. Hillary sped up his pace.

Arriving there, the situation was out of control. Charles was standing in a corner of the ward like a scared animal. There was blood on his hospital gown and splashed on the walls, as well as on his bed. There was a female nurse knocked out in the floor and two male nurses surrounding Charles and trying to talk with him. His grimace was, however, of fierce hate. He was ready to start fighting with the nurses when he saw Dr. Hillary.

His face immediately changed. He displayed preoccupation and shame. Dr. Hillary started talking kindly with him and the nurses were able to get closer by following Dr. Hillary with careful steps. Dr. Hillary was asking Charles' permission to give him an injection. He was already offering his shoulder to let Dr. Hillary apply the syringe in his arm when two security guards entered the room. Charles slapped Dr. Hillary's face and moved toward the nurses. The security guards jumped toward him and the four men immobilized Charles on the ground. Dr. Hillary injected the medication in his deltoid muscle. A few minutes later, Charles was sound asleep. Dr. Hillary told the nurses to transfer Charles to the ICU.

When Dr. Hillary left the room, he met Jill crying outside. The ward head nurse had held her outside of the room, protecting her from the depressing scene occurring inside. Dr. Hillary approached her and said, "Jill, I will have to talk with you later. Please go to the cafeteria. I will meet you there in about a half-hour. I have to see the patient I operated on today. I will ask Greg to meet you there while you wait for me."

He left without giving her time to speak.

The head nurse of the psychiatric ward called Jill to her office and talked with her. She calmed her down and asked her if she needed a medication to feel better. Jill rejected saying that she really needed to talk with Dr. Hillary. She left to the cafeteria when she saw that Charles was deeply asleep and ready to be transported to the neurosurgery intensive care unit. They had already replaced his I.V., changed his clothes, and cleaned his bed. Charles was with a peaceful appearance. A tear came from her right eye; she wiped it and turned to leave the room. When she walked through the door, she saw Greg walking in her direction with a worried face.

"What is going on, Jill?"

"It was Charles in one of his rage episodes."

"Yes, I was checking the CT scan of the nurse he knocked out. Thank God nothing happened, it was just a small concussion. She is already awake, actually remembering all that happened. Dr. Hillary asked me to take you the cafeteria and keep you company while he sees his patient. Let's go."

Chapter 32
Why?

"Where were you, Jill? I looked for you all day long. I almost gave up on you. I was just tying some loose ends before going home when Dr. Hillary paged me. He asked me to keep you company while he went to check the post-operative scan of his today's patient. He also had to talk with the patient's relatives before he could be here in the cafeteria with you."

"Greg, you don't need to keep me company. Your shift has finished, you should go home and rest. I am work for you; you should not work beyond your weekly 80 hours. You told me that recently."

"One cannot be a neurosurgeon working only 80 hours per week. You are kidding, spending time with you is not work for me. Moreover, I feel so bad about this morning. I added one more preoccupation to your already almost unbearable problem."

"It's fine; I already settled it, Greg."

"I told Dr. Hillary that I informed you about Randy's hypothalamic hamartoma. He was worried that you would think that he withheld the truth from you. He did however explain me why he was waiting to tell you. He also went on to give me a long lecture on how to break news to patient's families. You know Dr. Hillary when he starts on his professorial mode."

"I sure know, Greg. Thanks anyway for taking the time to talk with me. I guess Dr. Hillary wants to talk with me tonight about Randy's prognosis. He must think that I am worried mad."

"Do you have any questions about hypothalamic hamartoma? It is a benign tumor, don't worry."

"I spent the day at the library; I read all I could put my hands on about hamartomas, textbooks and scientific papers, all. I am actually confused on what will happen to Randy, but we have plenty of time to discuss our course of action. There is no good form of treatment."

"You must have learned a lot, you are already talking like Dr. Hillary, Jill."

"It's rubbing on. I spent too much time with him this past 3 weeks," answered Jill, now more relaxed.

"I think hamartomas can be removed. It is difficult surgical approach to arrive where they are, but a good neurosurgeon using the microscope may be able to remove them completely," Greg tried to comfort Jill further.

"No Greg, it is extremely rare that they can be completely removed. The incidence of visual, memory, and hormonal complications is very high in all published series I could find. After surgery, patients end up with a lot of troubles and many times still have the seizures, which is the reason why hypothalamic hamartomas are operated on. Patients may develop mental retardation with time if they are not managed properly. Seizures must be controlled."

"Mostly, they have short period of unawareness of the environment, or uncontrolled involuntary laughing or even generalized seizures. We don't know as yet how Randy's symptoms will evolve. Hopefully, he will have seizures only when his threshold for neuronal firing in the brain decreases, as it is the case of a febrile state. Fevers are readily controlled with medication, so I am hopeful that Randy will evolve without problems and grow up as a normal child. At this point, I believe the best measure is a watchful waiting. I expect that this is what Dr. Hillary will tell me today."

"You definitely know more about hamartomas than I do. I haven't had the chance to read about it as yet. I just remember a patient I followed in the ward when I was an intern. He had a terrible diabetes insipidus after the operation, urinating nonstop. It took time for him to start to retain water and maintain his hydration. He was discharged three weeks after his operation. I don't know about his final outcome."

"Greg, this story is not very encouraging, but I am realistic about Randy's situation. At this moment, Charles' problems are so much more pressing than Randy's that I have to accept that Dr. Hillary was just protecting me from one more worry."

"You must be right; anyway, how can I help you in your quest to help Charles? I understand that you have a lot of data analyses to do. I will be out of the clinical service starting next week. I finished my block of clinical rotations. As part of my residence training, I will have six months of research starting after spring break. I would love to get involved in your research and help Charles' cause. After talking with Dr. Hillary and seeing your struggle to help him, I feel compelled to study behavioral surgery. You are living an incredible drama."

"Yes, I need a lot of help. I have more data to analyze than I can handle. Moreover, you have much more knowledge of brain anatomy than I do. If I can put myself together, this coming weekend I will be reviewing the imaging data that I acquired in my primate experiments using the new software that Dr. Hillary's medical physics group just bought. It will be a great help if you start helping me. My computer knowledge is very limited. Charles always helped me when I got stuck; he is so good with computers."

"I do understand computers, but they are not my cup of tea. I did a doctorate in philosophy studying molecular biology. My intention was to complete neurosurgery and continue my research on novel therapies for malignant brain tumors. The reality is that I am so fascinated by Dr. Hillary's research that I am considering changing my research direction."

"Greg, as you know, I am developing my doctorate thesis on brain imaging obtained on different states of its function, mostly as it pertains to a primate's aggressive behavior. You can imagine why."

"Sure I understand. I would study the same if I had a specimen in my home." Immediately, Greg apologized.

"It is OK, Greg. I am questioning myself why I put up with such a mess. I married this sick man, now my whole life is going to hell."

"Oh Jill, sorry I brought you to this mood."

"It was not you, Greg, I spent the past three weeks on this mood. I have lost three weeks of classes, my son has a very complicated illness, my husband is involved in a crime and here I am dreaming of being a medical doctor and a scientist. Am I realistic?"

Luckily, at this moment Dr. Hillary entered in the cafeteria. The conversation was getting way beyond Greg's head. He was a good young doctor in training, but still without experience to deal with a problem of Jill's magnitude.

Dr. Hillary asked, smiling, "How are you kids doing?"

Greg stood up and said: "I am fine, but ready to go home. I had a hell of a day. I will start tomorrow with rounds at 5 AM."

Greg was afraid of continuing talking and making matters with Jill even worse. He knew he had brought terrible feelings to her when he made his insensitive remark of Charles being an aggressive primate specimen. He was feeling so stupid, why was he demeaning Charles? Maybe it was because of the long day of work and because he really liked Jill and wanted to help her. He felt very inadequate, he knew so little about hamartomas and on top of his ignorance, he came up with that terrible remark about Charles.

"Thanks for keeping company with Jill; I was very worried about her. Sorry it took me so long to come. That patient I operated on today developed a post-operative hematoma in the tumor bed; I had to take her back to the operating room to wash the clot out. The worst part is that she can't move her right side. I hope she will improve. Jill, I will grab something to eat and come back for us to talk. Bye, Greg."

"Bye, Dr. Hillary. Bye, Jill," said Greg and left Jill alone.

Chapter 33
Confession

Dr. Hillary returned with a huge plate of pasta and a cup of coffee. He hadn't eaten since early morning. The day had been so busy that he had no time to eat. He sat opposite Jill and started eating and listened to Jill's description of what she had learned about hamartomas in the library. She conveyed to him that she understood the seriousness of Randy's disease. She also let him know that she understood his attitude of sparing her from this difficult news, since there was nothing to do at this moment about the hamartomas and she was already so overwhelmed with the sequence of events with Charles.

She finally opened up to him her frustration about the course that her life was taking. She was having hard time to accept that she missed three weeks of classes. She had to finish her degree as soon as possible because of her and Charles' financial situation, mainly now that Charles' mother had also to take off work to help with Charles. She felt lucky that her mother could stay with Randy in San Diego, but she knew that this situation was temporary. She was unsure if she would be able to complete the semester successfully; she already knew she would have a major drop in her grades.

She also communicated to Dr. Hillary her skepticism with the possibility of obtaining any breakthrough in the next few weeks to be able to help Charles with surgery. He was obviously not being able to control himself even to be left awake in the psychiatric ward. She was in a swirl of anxiety. She was speaking nonstop about all her negative thoughts when Dr. Hillary interrupted her as he had finished his plate of pasta and was now sipping his coffee.

"Jill, calm down. We will take one thing at a time. You are correct about Randy and your understanding of hamartomas, there is nothing we should do now, so let him with your mother until we settle Charles' matter."

"Ok, but do you have any great idea on how we will settle Charles' matter?"

"Obviously, I don't have the final answer now, but I have a course of action that will at least allow you to finish this semester successfully and proceed with your research work toward your doctorate. You are almost finishing the basic course work, which is common for your medical degree and your doctorate in philosophy. I suggest that you finish this course work the best way you can. There is only one quarter to go. Then you take at least the coming school year off to do the research necessary to compile the data for your doctorate thesis."

"We will fashion your thesis to hinge on Fred's and Charles' brain imaging data. During this coming year, we will have to collect some brain imaging data from control subjects, such as your medical student colleagues. You can match their age and sex with Charles easily. I believe that you will be able to write a thesis acceptable for a doctorate degree in neurosciences with the differences you will find between the normal subjects, Charles's and that of Fred's brains."

"Dr. Hillary, this will not settle Charles' matter, it will just postpone my medical degree and more, make our financial situation unbearable."

"Jill, I am trying to organize your studies first. I understand that this is your major cause of frustration right now. As the high achiever that you are, you cannot accept not to complete the challenge you posed to yourself. Obviously, you and I miscalculated the severity of Charles' disease. These recent events call for a major rearrangement of our plans. Please listen to me until I finish, then we can modify the plans according to your reasoning and suggestions. Now, you are just a pile of anxiety and confusion, please go get a cup of coffee and return ready to listen to all I have to say."

Dr. Hillary needed a break to organize his thoughts. He felt responsible for the mess Jill was finding herself in. He was wondering if he should have advised that young couple to take so much responsibility at once. It was becoming clear to him that Charles had broken down and now Jill was on the verge of doing the same. He had to come up with a plan of action that was acceptable to Jill and at the same time effective for her to achieve her dreams. She was that type of person who would be very unhappy if she did not complete her studies. Moreover, with Charles' situation, he was not seeing him continuing his studies, or even contributing to society any time soon.

Jill walked back with her cup of coffee.

"Did you calm down?" asked Dr. Hillary, smiling.

"How can I? Everything is happening so fast! Actually, the day spent in the library today was the best day I had in a long time."

"Yes, because you concentrated on a single problem. You were able to isolate Randy's disease and immerse yourself on it. You used your brain in a focused manner, in such a way that you were able to relax about the problem. You did it despite the severity of the issue. You have to do the same regarding Charles."

"Sorry to say this, but I am already starting to think that was a mistake marrying Charles. I knew all along about his disease, it was naïve of me to think that I could surmount a problem of this magnitude."

"Jill, when we are young and full of energy, we think we can face any problem. You are extremely intelligent, gifted in so many ways and more, able to truly love. You dedicated all this accumulated talent to help Charles. This is natural, mostly when you look back and remember how promising Charles always was as an athlete and student."

"If I am as intelligent as you are trying to make me believe, I would have seen the writing on the wall that Charles sooner or later would get himself into a major problem."

"Jill, we went through this before. We planned Charles' life together to avoid problems. Now, we know that we failed in this regard, but it does not mean that we have lost the battle. As I told you before, it will take a major change on our plans and the use of all your talents. Jill, I know that life has been hard on you, and possibly you are thinking it is unfair, but it may look also unfair to others that you are gifted with so much talent. Life tends to ask more from the gifted ones. It is possible that the gifted ones naturally take more on themselves to carry the less privileged ones. Or maybe the gifted people feel happy only when they are applying all their talents. The reality is that you are one of these gifted people."

"Now, you have to handle the fact that you took on yourself a major responsibility. You trusted me when I told you that Randy, 'your bundle of love', would just help bring out the best in you and Charles. I feel somewhat responsible, because although you have maintained yourself on a high productive level, Charles was not able to keep the same pace and actually broke down. Therefore, I will be with you until we resolve all these issues we are facing. You will have to have confidence in me and I will have to use all my experience and knowledge to support you in your dreams. Together, we can resolve this mess."

"Dr. Hillary, you should not feel that you are responsible for my problems, you probably have a slew of your own at home."

"I don't, but I did. Luckily, I found someone to help me. Now I want to be that person for you until you are well oriented and with your life flowing smoothly."

"Was it a teacher that helped you?"

"No, at that time, it was a professional I sought for help. She was recommended to me because I needed psychological help. She became my wife and helped me to raise my children through their teens. Now we have all the time in the world. She is no longer a psychologist but a writer. I was progressively able to return to the same pace of neurosurgery I practice today."

"You are needing psychological help, I don't believe."

"Yes, at that time I was starting as a neurosurgeon here, I had already four children; I married in my first year of medical school. My youngest son was mentally retarded and very aggressive, actually self-destructive. My wife of 20 years then decided that it was too much for her and left me with the four children. I had to take three months off work to organize my home and my mind. It was during that period that I met my current wife, my shrink then. She understood my dilemma; she was attractive and sympathetic to my profession. She understood well the brain and my research interest. Unfortunately, my son committed suicide when he was 15 years old. My other three children are now in college. The oldest decided to go to medical school. I have to work this hard because of the high college bills I have to pay."

"I hope to slow down and dedicate the majority of my time to this very research we are doing now when my children finish college. I started this line of research trying to solve my late son's disease. It is unfortunate, however, that there is so little money for this line of research. You have already experienced the frustration of preparing an excellent research grant application to obtain government funding and see it rejected."

"The government invests so much into wars, research in AIDS, cancer, stroke and trauma, but has forgotten this important societal problem. Much of the violence in the streets and the full prisons could be solved if proper funding was dispensed for studies in this arena. Sorry Jill, I lost the track of our conversation to digress in this long confession."

"It is OK, Dr. Hillary. I am amazed to hear so much about your life that you had never let out."

"Yes, I don't like to remember all this, but I thought it would be useful for you to understand that I have been through very difficult times but now it is all fine. It is important for us to rely on the ones offering help when all seems so bleak. So, please feel free to call me anytime. I have a personal interest in helping you. Now, let's return to your problems."

Chapter 34
Plan of Action

Jill and Dr. Hillary continued talking way past midnight. They decided that they would obtain Charles' scans in the sedated and at rage moment in the next three days. After that, Jill would train Greg to transfer Fred's and Charles' brain images to the new software for analysis. During this transfer period, Jill would finish her quarter and prepare for taking one year off for research. During that year she would acquire the needed control data from medical students' brain and start writing her thesis. The only unresolved point was how to handle Charles while they didn't know where to target him with surgery. This was important, because someone needed to care for Charles until they could operate on him. Dr. Hillary suggested that they talk with Dr. Bernard about the ECT. It could help by completely depolarizing Charles brain, exhausting the neurotransmitters and hopefully triggering a new control of his brain if proper drugs were associated to the ECT. In other words, reboot his brain.

"Dr. Hillary, you don't think that the ECT will damage Charles' brain. I heard that the memory becomes compromised when ECT is repeated many times."

"Hopefully we will be able to find the surgical solution for Charles soon to avoid repetition of ECT. We will have to discuss with Dr. Bernard about harmful effects of ECT. Now let's go check on Charles in the ICU before we go home."

"No Dr. Hillary, we still did not solve the financial problem. We don't have money to last more than one year if Charles stops making his graduate student salary."

"I will take upon myself to find funds for you. I will ask donation from a personal friend of mine that understands the power of destruction of uncontrollable rage. He is a successful business man whose son is confined to one of his vacation homes for the past 15 years. He maintains full-time nurses to care for him. This is his only son, I will convince him to invest in you as if he was paying for the education of his son. You will have to meet with him and explain your story. You have to commit to offer similar therapy to his son as you find the solution for Charles' disease. I am sure that he will be sympathetic and hopeful when he meets your passion to your research."

"I feel funny about this type of donation, Dr. Hillary. Looks like that I am begging."

"Don't feel so, Jill. What you are doing is offering hope to this man and his son based on your knowledge, passion and energy. You have a great future ahead of you and almost certainty that you will find the solution for his son's problems; a solution he has sought for more than 15 years. You are actually offering a noble way for him to spend his money."

"I wouldn't go that far," chuckled Jill.

"You would be surprised. Financially successful people feel frequently empty after they achieve a level of finances that they have no more drive to make money. They want to employ their money in some noble cause. It makes them feel good about themselves and decreases the amount of taxes they pay to the government. They usually try to employ their excess money to a cause that they identify with in their personal lives. This man cannot see a better way to spend his money. So please make a reasonable budget for you to finish your studies, including day care for

Randy. We will present him with the problem. I would like to set a day for you to meet him as soon as possible. It all will depend on his availability. Cross your fingers Jill."

"Thank you, Dr. Hillary, I will prepare for the meeting. Now, can we go see Charles in the ICU?"

Standing in front of the ICU door were two armed policemen.

Chapter 35
Grandma and the Net

Randy had three more seizures while under the care of Jill's mother. She took him to the emergency room in San Diego. There the doctors confirmed that he had a small abnormality in the hypothalamus. This abnormality was readily seen in touch with his optical nerve. They also confirmed that the seizures only happened when Randy's temperature was high. He had a recurrence of his urinary infection because Jill's mother, who was not in the medical field, thought that his antibiotic therapy was completed. She also got confused with the seizure medication, so she called Charles' mother to help her.

Since Charles was in the intensive care unit, his mother returned to San Diego, where she was more needed. The doctors in San Diego were talking about operating on Randy to remove the hamartoma. They were promising cure of the seizures. This brought confusion to Jill's and Charles' mothers. They were so worried about the fate of the young couple. They both were under pressure on their job. Their husbands were also confused regarding how to proceed. They didn't know if they would ask their wives to take off work to care for Randy. They were actually tempted to accept the idea of surgery, thinking that it could solve part of the young couple's problem.

Charles' father typed hamartomas on the internet and found a number of sites offering the perfect treatment for the disease. Even well-known universities were offering microsurgical resection with the promise of full cure. Obviously, there was no mention of the complications of the surgery. He printed all he could find in support of surgery, invited Jill's father, and both left for Los Angeles to speak with Jill. They wanted to convince her to accept the surgery in San Diego.

Charles' mother, who had already talked to Dr. Hillary and Jill, advised them that they were wasting their time. She said that Jill had read all she could find about hamartomas and had made her mind about Randy's treatment. Jill's mother, however, encouraged her husband to talk with their daughter. She knew of Jill's open-minded nature and wanted her to know that they were at her side, trying to help her all the way.

Grandma was dedicated to Randy's care and as a layperson, she thought that what was written on the internet was worth looking at. She had heard of too many stories of patients that had been turned down in major centers and found the cure by following what they found on the net. Randy was such a healthy looking boy; she didn't want to accept that he would have to carry through life a health problem that was potentially curable.

Chapter 36
Policemen!

"Policemen! Why?" asked Jill when she was stopped at the ICU door.

"They are probably here to ensure that Charles does not run away," answered Dr. Hillary.

"This is ridiculous; they should be here to take the other fellow to jail. I am sure that Charlie was provoked by those two fellows," said Jill, disgusted.

"I am sure you are right, but all evidence is against Charles. It will be only his word against the comatose fellow's word! I bet you that a good lawyer would generate a lot of pity against Charles in front of a jury," said Dr. Hillary.

"Charles' past police reports will definitely not help him. He will be seen as a dangerous fellow who should be locked up for lifetime, as I always feared."

"Calm down, Jill, the policemen are here just to follow the law. If I sign a paper that I am responsible for Charles' acts, they will go away," said Dr. Hillary.

"Are you willing to sign such a paper, Dr. Hillary?"

"No Jill, I don't think it is wise to sign anything. Charles has shown to be completely unpredictable. Moreover, if I get in trouble with the law, it will not help Charles or you. The policemen do not bother me, do they bother you?"

"No, they don't bother me; it is just so outrageous that they are here watching Charles when real criminals are running free."

"I agree, but it is to our advantage that they are here. They will protect Charles or people that he can hurt if he gets out of control. After what happened today in the ward, I feel more comfortable with the policemen here."

"What do you mean?" asked Jill.

"Charles hit me when I was trying to give him an injection to calm him down."

"I'm sorry, Dr. Hillary, I am sure that Charles didn't mean hitting you."

"I'm sure he meant it, Jill, he was quite conscious when he did. He felt like a cornered animal and was afraid of the security guards. I thought a lot about it, mainly after I talked with you tonight about my guilty feelings and participation in the events happening to you and Charles. Maybe I deserve it. I could have advised you, Charles or both to take it easy when you informed me you were having a child. Instead, I encouraged you to take as much work as possible because you were young and could handle it all."

"Looks like I didn't learn from my own past experiences. My troubles were different from yours, but they should have taught me that neurosurgery and science monopolize completely ones' time. Rarely one has time for family life when this combination is put together. Neurosurgery alone is enough to destroy relationships. It is difficult for the lay person to understand the dedication of a neurosurgeon. They only accept what we do because they think we make a lot of money, but the reality is that comparing the number of hours we work with the regular working person, and the amount of sacrifice we impose on ourselves and our families, we neurosurgeons make actually very little money. It is even more outrageous with the current academic salaries."

"Dr. Hillary, this is not very encouraging for a woman dreaming of becoming a researcher and a neurosurgeon."

"Sorry Jill, we are both overtired. It is time to go home and have some rest. Work brings depression only when it is too much and without breaks. An overly tired person is a sick person. Charles will need us healthy the next few days. We will need all our wits to acquire the data we need to help him. Have a good night!"

"Goodnight, Dr. Hillary, I want to kiss Charlie before I go home."

Charles was peacefully asleep in the ICU bed. The monitors were showing stable vital signs and his brain electrical waves (Electroencephalogram, EEG) were denoting a peaceful sleep pattern of neuronal firing.

Chapter 37
Old Times

Jill arrived home at midnight to find her father and father-in-law watching a soccer game on her living room TV set. They were reviewing old videos of Charles' plays in the World Cup. Each had a beer bottle half drunk and seemed very relaxed. When they saw Jill entering the door, they immediately turned the TV set off and stood up. Jill's father hugged her. She let all her tiredness of the day in his arms. Her body relaxed when she felt his embrace. She needed so much that love contact. Charles' dad did the same guiding her toward the sofa. She set down, took her shoes off, closed her eyes and enjoyed the familiar feeling of home and loved ones around.

"Jill," started her father, "we are here to discuss Randy's surgery."

"Which surgery?" asked Jill, standing up and gazing them with her big dark eyes.

"Dr. Winslow, a neurosurgeon from La Jolla, wants to remove Randy's hamartoma. He assures that he can cure Randy's seizures."

"Sorry Father, I am too tired to discuss this with you now, but surgery is not an option at this moment. Goodnight!"

"No Jill, listen to us," said Charles's father. "We have done a full search on the net; surgery is the best option for Randy."

"No, you are not telling me that you came to discuss internet medical recommendations after the day I have had. The least I need now is laypeople using advertisements from the net to direct my son's medical care. Sorry, but this is the last thing I need now." She covered her face and started sobbing.

She lay down on the sofa and cried. She wouldn't stop crying. The two men didn't know what to do or say, like men get when women start crying. They felt so awkward and out of place. They could not understand Jill's reaction. Her father tried to embrace her again, but she pushed him away; she sobbed and sobbed until she entered into a deep slumber. The two men looked at each other without knowing if they should return to San Diego or wait for her to wake up. They finally decided to stay and talk with her again the next day. Her father covered her with a blanket and invited Charles' father to the kitchen. Each made a sandwich, sat, and finished their beer, eating in silence.

One finally broke the silence, "I don't understand, we thought we were helping. We spent so much time preparing ourselves for this conversation. What do you think went wrong?"

"I don't know; we brought such a wealth of information to discuss with her. Why is she so averse to discuss Randy's care?"

"Do you think she is in denial about Randy's disease?"

"I don't know. I am no psychologist. I would rather think that she is overtired and depressed about all that is going on. Let's go to sleep, tomorrow we talk to her again."

When they woke up next morning, Jill had already left for the hospital. She had slept three hours and had gone back to see Charles. The two men couldn't believe that she didn't even look over the information they had left at the coffee table close to the sofa where Jill was sleeping. Frustrated, they decided to have breakfast in the hospital cafeteria, planning to visit Charles and hoping to find Jill for one more attempt to discuss Randy's need for surgery.

While they were having breakfast, Jill and Dr. Hillary entered the cafeteria talking about the first PET they were planning for Charles. Jill's father interrupted them with a good morning greeting.

Jill kissed him and introduced him to Dr. Hillary.

"Nice meeting you, I have been curious to meet the father of this smart girl. You are lucky; she will be a great doctor."

"Thank you, please meet Charles' father."

"I am pleased to meet you too. I guess you are here to visit Charles. We will take you up to the ICU after we have something to eat. We are coming from there, Charles is fine and sound asleep."

"Thank you, but we also want to talk to Jill about our grandson's surgery."

"Surgery?" questioned Dr. Hillary looking at Jill.

"Internet doctors," Jill said with a smile.

Dr. Hillary looked at them and said, "Let's sit and talk. I want to learn what you have to say, maybe in this conversation we can come up with a plan for Randy."

"Great!" Jill's father said, looking at Dr. Hillary's eyes. "Now we found someone with sense," and started: "Dr. Winslow from La Jolla recommended surgery for Randy's tumor. What do you think about it, Dr. Hillary?"

"I disagree, but he must have his reasons. Did he discuss with you the reason for surgery and the risks of surgery in such a delicate area of the brain?"

"He said he can cure Randy's seizures with one surgery. Do you know him, Dr. Hillary?"

"Yes, I know him very well. I have seen many of his patients coming to me for a second opinion. I almost invariably disagree with him. But why does he want to operate on such a young child? We don't even know if the seizures will persist."

"They are persisting; Randy had a bout of them, this is the reason why we took him to the emergency room in San Diego and why Dr. Winslow came into the picture. Moreover, he said that the tumor will grow, and the seizures will worsen. He also said that Randy's vision will deteriorate, and he will become mentally retarded if surgery is not performed."

"This is not true," cut Jill anxiously. "I spent a day reading at the library and can assure you that what Dr. Winslow is saying is incorrect."

"Jill, aren't you just listening to what you want to listen to?" asked her father.

"No Father, I read the papers myself. Actually, we had such a busy time around Charles' disease that Dr. Hillary and I have yet to discuss plans for Randy."

"Jill, let's take advantage that your parents are here and let's talk about the management of Randy's hamartoma. What do you think?"

"Fine with me, it is just that we have so much to do in preparation for Charles' scans that I hate to waste time now and in the next three days."

"Jill, I think that your parents need to know our plans, otherwise these two poor guys will go crazy trying to digest all the information they read on the net, and mostly because now their confusion is aggravated by two doctors' diverging opinions. When I talked with you briefly about Randy last night, I understood that you had correctly concluded that we need to wait for the course of Randy's seizures before we make a decision of treating his hamartoma. Is it true?" asked Dr. Hillary.

"Yes," answered Jill.

"So, what is this story that Randy's seizures are persisting in spite of the medication?"

"I talked with Mom over the phone yesterday. She stopped giving Randy's antibiotics and seizures medications for three days. He had fever and ended up in the emergency room at Scripts Clinic."

"Well, so the seizures are the same we saw here when he had fever from his urinary infection."

"Correct," said Jill's father. "My wife misunderstood the pediatrician's order when Randy was discharged. Dr. Winslow said however that the growth of the hamartoma will only make Randy's seizures worse."

"I believe that Dr. Winslow is painting the picture worse than it really is. He is trying to bring Randy into surgery. Let me explain to you how Randy's hamartoma is so you can understand where I am coming from," said Dr. Hillary.

"Please," said Jill's father.

"Randy has a 5 mm in diameter abnormality seen on a very detailed MRI scan I ordered because I suspected by analyzing his CT scan that his hypothalamus, the area in the brain controlling hormones, behavior, and other important functions, was slightly deformed. Therefore this 5 mm hamartoma is completely attached to the floor of his hypothalamus touching his optic nerve from above. The surgical access to this region is very difficult. Moreover, the hamartoma is almost a continuum with the hypothalamus, involving extremely important hormonal functions of Randy's body. Growth, mental development, sexual definition, control of food intake and memory are all intimately related to the hypothalamus and consequently to Randy's hamartoma."

"A surgery in that area would most likely destroy his ability to develop as a normal boy. At this time, our best bet is control the seizures with medication and observe his development. We also need to keep a close eye on his hormones. We will find a pediatric endocrinologist to follow him with us."

"What do you think about Dr. Winslow's assertion that the hamartoma will grow and compromise Randy's vision?"

"It won't, because hamartomas do not grow, they are just a displacement of neural cells that may become hyper excitable leading to seizures," helped Jill.

"Correct," confirmed Dr. Hillary and continued, "Since these cells do not multiply like regular tumor cells, the only harm they cause is the seizures. Now, Dr. Winslow is correct when he said that Randy's mental development can be compromised. But this only will happen if we cannot control the seizures with medication. If we fail to control his seizures with medication, I would treat Randy's hamartoma with radiosurgery."

"What kind of surgery is this?" asked Charles' father.

"These days, we can focus an extremely high dose of radiation delivered by converging beams with the precision of a pencil dot. This high dose of radiation concentrated on the hamartoma's cells renders these dysfunctional cells silent, unable to generate electrical activity. The seizures are therefore completely controlled in this way."

Jill interrupted, "You had not mentioned this possibility to me."

"I didn't because it was not necessary at the time we talked, and we were really concentrated on Charles' recent behavior. Do you have any questions?" asked Dr. Hillary to Jill and the two old men.

"Why don't you perform radiosurgery now? It seems so simple and effective," Jill's father asked.

"We could if the situation was indeed out of control. All surgical procedures carry risks. Randy would have to be under general anesthesia, taking its risks. There is also a minor amount of radiation that would go to his hypothalamus and pituitary gland. This minor amount of radiation could potentially affect his growth hormone, the one that is most sensitive to radiation. Therefore, I feel that we should run these risks only when it becomes necessary. It is a matter of being extra careful with Randy's care."

"Sirs, unfortunately, I will have to go. I have a surgery starting in few minutes; I still need to explain the surgery to the patient's family. Jill, please continue talking with them. It was a pleasure meeting both of you. Bye!"

Chapter 38
Sleeping Brain

Jill had a lot of logistics to arrange before a PET scan could be obtained from Charles' sleeping brain. Dr. Hillary asked her to prepare all that was necessary so the scan could be done that afternoon as soon as he could leave from the operating room. Dr. Hillary wanted to be present during the scans to ensure they were obtained correctly. He also wanted to show his interest to the PET scan doctors; they were doing the scans for free as a courtesy to him. All had to be expedited because Charles' medical insurance didn't want to pay for his stay in the ICU or the scans. They couldn't find in their manuals that patients with Charles' disease needed PET scans or be admitted to the ICU.

Now, Charles was considered a patient with a chronic psychiatric disease. Dr. Hillary would have to pull a lot of strings to gather the data collection necessary to design a surgical procedure for Charles. Moreover, he would also have to find private funds to pay the hospital expenses related to surgery, because the insurance would not cover such an unknown surgery. Insurances would always try to find a good reason not to pay the patients' bills. This surgery would be an easy denial for them.

Jill left her parents at the ICU door after taking them to visit Charles. The men thanked Jill and apologized for taking so much of Dr. Hillary's and her time. She accepted the apologies and thanked them for their efforts and for generating the opportunity to discuss in such much detail Randy's situation. She also thanked them for the care they were giving to Randy. She promised to take him back to Los Angeles during her summer vacation, when she would have already settled Charles' pressing issues and had finished the school quarter. She told them of her plan to take off one year to complete her research, generate the data for her doctorate thesis, and for Charles possible surgery. They embraced her and left happily for home with their good deed.

Jill entered the ICU where Greg was seeing patients and told him of Dr. Hillary's plan to take Charles under complete sedation to the PET scanner. She said that Dr. Hillary had asked her to recruit his help to organize Charles' transportation to the basement of the research building where the scanner was located. She told him that she was going to work with Dr. Larsson and Mallory on the generation of the radioactive compounds to inject in Charles' veins before performing the scans. She left Greg with his tasks and ran to the laboratory to meet with Dr. Larsson.

"Jill, you look tired," greeted Dr. Larsson.

"Yes, neurosurgery or life of a crazy man's wife, pick one. I had only three hours of sleep last night. We need to take advantage of the fact that Charles is in the ICU and perform the scans while he is asleep. Sorry to impose this on you, Dr. Larsson, but our insurance is denying his stay in the ICU. We will have to transfer him to the psychiatric ward tomorrow."

"I understand that crazy professor of yours woke me up past midnight to tell me you would need the radioactive drugs this afternoon. He has no idea on what is involved to prepare these drugs. I came 5 am today to organize the laboratory and arrange the chemicals necessary. I also had to talk the cyclotron people into preparing the isotopes for me. It was not easy to convince them to fit such a request in their day. They are nine-to-five people with no understanding of medical necessities. Well, it is all done; we will have the isotopes as soon as you bring Charles down. Just give me a half-hour notice, I will be there when you need me."

"Thank you, Dr. Larsson, you know you are doing this for me and Charles. Our crazy professor is also doing the best he can to help us. I can't believe that that man can sleep so little, do so much and still keep his good mood. I guess he loves what he does," said Jill.

"Do you think that this scan will be more complicated than the ones we did for Fred?" asked Dr. Mallory, who was overhearing the conversation while he worked on his computer pulling Fred's experiment procedures.

"The scan we are performing today will be easy because the anesthesiologist will be with us keeping Charles' sedation level under control. The one tomorrow will be another story. I am afraid to wake up Charles as he has been so unpredictable since his admission. I will need to discuss the procedures with Dr. Hillary, and we still didn't have the time to sit down to talk. He told me that he wants to discuss the details for tomorrow after the today's scan when all will be present, including Dr. Bernard."

"Why do we need Dr. Bernard today in the scanner room?"

"I passed by his office just before I came here to let him know that Dr. Hillary was asking him to be at the scanner this afternoon. Dr. Bernard asked me the same question. I guess Dr. Hillary knows the answer. Let's see what he says this afternoon. I am glad we are all on the same page. I will see you around 3 PM in the scanner. Dr. Hillary's surgery will be finishing around lunchtime. Bye!"

Chapter 39
Sleeping and Awake

Jill went to the operating room where Dr. Hillary was to coordinate with her and Greg Charles' transportation. Dr. Hillary was making the last stitch in the chest of the patient where he had just fished implanting a pulse generator to deliver electrical impulses to the patient's vagal nerve. He had wired the nerve to the generator in an attempted to treat the patient's severe depression. Jill approached him as he was taking his surgical gloves off to ask about the transportation plans. Dr. Hillary asked her to wait for him to finish the surgical report dictation and asked her to page Greg to the cafeteria where they would discuss their afternoon activities.

The conversation in the cafeteria was brief. Dr. Hillary had to see patients in clinic starting at one and still swap in a pulse generator in one patient. He didn't want to be late for Charles' scan at three. Dr. Hillary insisted with Greg that he wanted Charles at the research PET room at 3 PM sharp because of the short life of the isotopes used to prepare the neurotransmitters. The tagged epinephrine and serotonin were to be injected in Charles circulation while still radioactive. The anesthesiologist need to be informed of the need to be on time, otherwise they wouldn't understand a rush at this time in the afternoon for a patient in the ICU who would be having a routine scan.

The anesthesia team captain needed to be convinced that this was an important scan. Dr. Hillary had already talked with him, and he had accepted to free one of his young anesthesiologists from the main operating room to go to the scanner at 3 PM sharp. It was critical that Greg also convinced the transport nurse that time was of essence. He needed to be with Charles until they arrived in the scanner, otherwise the plans could fall through. Jill was to be a sidekick solving any unpredictable logistic problem.

At 3 PM sharp, Charles' stretcher entered the scanner room. The whole team was assembled, and the experimental protocol was started. Dr. Mallory made sure that all vital signs were recorded continuously and monitored his computer to compare with the vital signs to be recorded the next day, when Charles would be allowed to wake up before the scan. Dr. Larsson brought the radioactive neurotransmitters and gave to the anesthesiologist with all recommendations to be extremely careful not to spill a drop, not only because of the potential health hazard to all personnel present, but also because of the expensive nature of the procedure to produce the isotopes. He doubted that he would be able to produce a new batch of tagged drugs on time for today if they were spilled.

The only member of the team not present was Dr. Bernard. Dr. Hillary noticed but proceeded with the plans. The anesthetist kept the anesthesia level light but enough to maintain Charles immobile. He would react slightly, however, to painful stimuli. His corneal reflexes were present showing how light he was on the anesthesia. His pupils were small. The radioactive neurotransmitters were injected, and the scan was obtained 10 minutes later. The whole procedure went perfectly, and Charles was transported back to the ICU, now deeper in his anesthesia.

The group continued in the anteroom of the PET scanner. Jill had brought a bag of cookies to keep all from leaving for coffee. The PET technician brewed a pot of coffee and Dr. Hillary started planning for the next day.

"Great job, team! The easy part of the data acquisition is over. Now we need to prepare ourselves for tomorrow. I really needed Dr. Bernard here for this meeting. He is a key person on the whole process tomorrow. I asked him to be here at three because I knew he would be late. Charles will have to be transported from here to the psychiatric ward. Dr. Bernard will have to have his plans settled to receive him there. I talked with him briefly about it but nothing is clearly established.”

Jill suggested: “Why don’t we discuss how to wake him up and the timing for injecting the tagged drugs just before the scan? We can discuss the post scans measures later.”

“Greg, could you please page Dr. Bernard to come here? We’ll take Jill’s suggestion.”

Dr. Hillary asked the anesthetist if he could come the next day at the same time. He answered that all would depend on the anesthesia team captain and asked: “Why do you need for me in particular? Any of us can keep the level of anesthesia the patient was maintained at today.”

“No, tomorrow we need to bring him just out of the anesthesia to a point where he becomes aggressive, and then we have to inject the tagged neurotransmitters. After the injection, we need to bring him down to the same level you kept him today during the scan. You are the only one that knows what you did today to accomplish this perfect anesthesia. We need to same level tomorrow because we need to compare the two scans for differences in neurotransmitter uptake throughout the brain. Any difference in the anesthesia level, which could happen if another anesthetist comes tomorrow, will add variables to our data. It would make the data analyses difficult, if not impossible.”

“Well, you will have to talk to our team captain again, I will be glad to come.”

At this moment, Dr. Bernard entered the room, very apologetic. “Sorry, I had an emergency in the ward. A kid nearly ate a roll of toilet paper, choked, and almost died. We had to call code blue. They placed an endotracheal tube, and we transferred him to the pediatric ICU.”

“Looks like you had a lot of fun! No harm done, now that we really need you. We are making the plans for tomorrow and wondering how you will keep Charles in your ward when he comes out of anesthesia,” said Dr. Hillary.

“When is he getting there?” asked Dr. Bernard.

“I believe that we will be done here between 4 and 5 PM. Charles will be then in a very superficial anesthesia, just enough to keep him from moving,” answered Dr. Hillary.

“Well, the anesthetist will have to bring him anesthetized to the ward and stay there until he becomes completely awake. If he acts aggressive as usual, the only way out I see is to give him an ECT and start him on high doses of narcoleptics. I will adjust the oral medication as he comes out of the immediate depression that the patients usually experience after the ECT.”

“Why do I need to be there waiting for him to wake up, you can give him the ECT when he arrives there still asleep, can’t you?” asked the anesthetist.

“No, I can’t, because you will have to give him muscle relaxants for us to proceed with the ECT. Therefore, you will have to place him in assisted ventilation. He has to have all his muscles paralyzed to avoid fractures that can happen during the massive electrical discharge that the ECT induces in the brain,” explained Dr. Bernard.

“Why do you think that ECT will help to control Charles’ aggressiveness, Dr. Bernard?” asked Jill.

“I don’t really know, but I count on the complete depletion of his neurotransmitters. Then I will induce a new state of function in his brain by manipulating gradually the antipsychotic drugs. I know, however, that he will be in a depressive state after the ECT, giving us in the ward a chance to organize his medical therapy. I wish we knew more about the effects of ECT to understand the reinstitution of the brain function after the massive discharge. Then we would be in a better position to enter with drugs to modulate the patient’s neurotransmitter repopulation,” Dr. Bernard answered awkwardly.

“What about the ECT side-effects?” Jill continued.

“The side-effects will be almost abolished if Charles is kept on muscle relaxants and deep sedation when we give the ECT. Repetition of ECT for years may lead to dullness and memory deficits. What we are planning here is only to keep Charles under control while Dr. Hillary and his crew put themselves together with their surgical plans,” remarked Dr. Bernard.

"Jill is the boss, as you know. We depend on her findings to devise a surgery for Charles," added Dr. Hillary.

"Wait a minute, I depend on you all and Greg has enlisted himself as a crew member," said Jill.

"Sorry Jill, tomorrow I will not be here because I will be after call," said Greg.

"You are kidding, forget about post call. We need you here and you will be here. See you tomorrow, Greg. Actually, see you all tomorrow. I am satisfied with Dr. Bernard's plans. Now I have to start another case in the operating room, my schedule was bumped until now by a patient with a gunshot wound in the head who arrived this morning. Bye."

All shook hands and left, thinking about their duties for the next day.

Chapter 40
Jealousy Again

Next day, the team was complete in the anteroom of the research PET scanner when Charles was wheeled in from the ICU. The anesthetist brought Charles' sedation to a superficial level. The corneal reflexes were present, the arterial blood pressure was stable and the pupils were small. Oxygen saturation, end titled carbon dioxide and breathing cycle were stable. Jill started talking with Charles. At the same moment, the anesthetist introduced the syringe containing the isotope tagged neurotransmitters in the three way I.V. line. He was prepared to inject the tagged drugs and sedate Charles immediately when necessary.

Charles opened his eyes and saw Jill. He opened up an immense smile. There were no changes in his vital signs, not even a change in his cardiac rate. He continued looking at her completely oblivious to the others in the room. He tried to say something she didn't understand. She came close to him and whispered in his ear: "What is it, Charlie?"

With difficulty, he uttered: "I love you," and smiled.

Jill held his hand and tried to explain to him that all was alright and that he was only undergoing a PET scan. The group was paralyzed. No one knew how to proceed. Dr. Hillary in the background was observing the scene and shaking his head to Dr. Mallory, assuming already the failure of the experiment. They needed Charles rage reaction at that moment to obtain the most important data to support his surgical strategy.

Dr. Larsson on the other side of the room looked at Greg and came up with one idea. While Jill was still talking with Charles, who was in the most passive mood he had since he left his home that terrible night, Dr. Larsson asked Greg to approach Jill from behind and look at Charles over Jill's head. Greg did not understand but followed Dr. Larsson's instruction.

As Greg approached Jill from behind and looked at Charles' eyes, the anesthetist noticed that the patient's cardiac rate was climbing. Jill also noticed Charles' pupils dilating and the arterial blood pressure suddenly skyrocketed. Dr. Hillary ordered the anesthesiologist to inject the tagged drugs. Charles started contorting his face with an angry expression and tried to sit up. He growled and screamed at Jill: "Don't do this to me; you are doing the same that you did with Fred."

The anesthetist injected the sedative; Charles relaxed and closed his eyes. Dr. Hillary checked the corneal reflex assuring it was present. The arterial blood pressure and the cardiac rate started to decrease. Charles was moved to the scanner.

Jill couldn't remain in the room. She left to the anteroom, sobbing. Dr. Larsson followed her and Greg stood in the room paralyzed. He didn't know what was going on. Dr. Hillary took charge and obtained the scans while Dr. Mallory recorded the data.

Jill continued crying while Dr. Larsson tried to console her. Greg continued looking at the scene asking Dr. Larsson what was going on. Why was Jill so shocked by Charles' words?

Dr. Mallory entered the anteroom observing the situation. He walked to Greg and told him to go home. He promised to explain everything to him next day, when he would return rested. Dr. Hillary walked toward Jill and Dr. Larsson; Dr. Bernard followed him.

When they approached her, she said: "Dr. Bernard, please don't give him the ECT. I will be there with him when the anesthesia wears off. I will calm him down."

"Jill, you will not be able to be with him twenty-four-seven. It is not realistic."

"I will ask his mother to come and help me. I will never forgive myself for letting Charlie suffer what he just demonstrated to me."

"Jill, he will not suffer. He will have retrograde and anterograde amnesia after the ECT," said Dr. Bernard.

"No, I will not sign the consent form. His parents have to come here to help me with this decision. Even if we have to keep him in the ICU, I will not carry with me the responsibility to give him ECT. His mother has avoided ECT for him during his entire life."

"OK Jill, I will call Charles' parents and explain the situation. Now you follow Dr. Bernard and the anesthetist with Charles to the psychiatric ward. If Charles wakes up out of control, we will transfer him to the ICU again and work from there," said Dr. Hillary.

"Thanks for understanding, Dr. Hillary. Dr. Larsson, would you go with us?" asked Jill.

"Sure, I will. If Charles wakes up calm and feels comfortable with my presence, I will take turns with you to keep him company until your mother-in-law arrives," said Dr. Larsson.

Chapter 41
New Analyst

Next morning, Dr. Hillary met Greg at 7 am in the cafeteria to explain to him the events of the previous afternoon and to encourage him to analyze the data acquired. He described to Greg the experiments that Jill had done with Fred three years before. He described Dr. Larsson's idea of having Charles stare into the monkey's eyes and the additional effect that Charles' presence had in making Fred aggressive during the identical experimental protocol followed the previous afternoon for Charles' scans while in a rage episode. Greg understood then that he was used to trigger a jealousy episode in Charles.

"But Dr. Hillary, there is nothing between me and Jill!" said Greg.

"Nobody is saying that there is. The reality is that Dr. Larsson is a very perceptive man. He saw that you may like Jill. Apparently, you like Jill enough for Charles' instincts to perceive it."

"What do you mean?" asked Greg, flushed and surprised.

"Greg, Charles is now in a very instinctive state. When someone acts in a rage episode, it is because the instinctive part of the brain has taken over the reasoning part. Obviously, Charles would be very ashamed of his reaction yesterday if he was on his usual self. Now forget about it. The experiment was successful thanks to your love for Jill. Now we need to use this love to help Jill and Charles."

"Stop pulling my leg, Dr. Hillary."

"I am not pulling your leg. You enlisted yourself as part of the team and want to help Jill, don't you?"

"Yes, but not for the reasons you are alluding to," said Greg.

"The reasons don't matter, what is important is that you now have time to involve yourself in an outstanding line of research. I need you to analyze the data obtained from Charles as soon as possible. I know that you will start your 6 months research rotation next Monday. Please get to work. I will introduce you to my medical physicists and you will have to find the differences on Charles' scans in the two states, sleeping and during rage."

"I will do my best, Dr. Hillary."

"We really need your full dedication because Jill most likely will be tied up with Charles. I heard that yesterday he woke up calm in her presence. She has always had a calming effect on him. Apparently, he does not remember yesterday's episode. The anesthetist had given him a drug that took his memory away during that period."

"Great, now I feel better, I hate to think that Charles would want to get me. His expression when he is irate is terrible," said Greg, smiling.

"As you know, Jill will have to continue her medical courses until the end of this quarter. Charles' mother, Mrs. Morales, and his father will be taking turns with Jill in the ward to keep Charles calm. Jill will have time to go to her classes and study while she is there with Charles and at home. I suggest that you never visit Charles, we don't want to disturb the nice recovery that we are seeing in him."

"Don't you worry, I never want to see his face in that state again," said Greg.

"I will visit them now. Would you like to help me in my operation this morning? If so, please position the patient for me in the operating room. I will be there soon."

"I'll do it," said Greg.

Chapter 42
Recovery

Charles had been docile now for 2 weeks. Jill was spending at least 10 hours per day with him. She would go to her classes and return immediately to the ward. Charles started reading love stories avidly. He was in good spirits and starting to ask Jill about Randy. He had not asked to go home, but he was slowly recovering his memory about the past. Jill was afraid that he would remember about the episode that happened in the alley and become aggressive again, but he seemed not to have a slight memory even of the event that happened in the apartment before he ran into the alley.

Charles' parents were alternating nights with Charles when Jill would go home and rest. Either Mr. or Mrs. Morales would cover her keeping Charles company when she went to her classes. They were managing to drive up and down from San Diego, work and help Jill. It was a major effort for both, but they were dedicated parents that were accustomed to sacrifice for Charles. He had a very demanding childhood and despite all the last events, they were very proud of Charles' accomplishments through life. They were very supportive of Jill's efforts and loved her as if she were their daughter. They admired her dedication and love for their son. They wanted to do everything necessary for her to succeed in medical school. They were also very hopeful that she would find the cure for their son's disease.

During the weeks that followed, Jill was able to catch up with her lost days at school and actually achieve outstanding grades. Her time with Charles in the ward was very productive. He was always reading and she was studying her subjects. They talked about Randy frequently. Charles was happy to know that Randy was being cared for by his mother. Charles had remembered enough of his past to understand that caring for Randy and for him would take Jill away from her studies. He started asking Jill when his doctor would allow him to return to his laboratory to continue his own studies.

Charles was so stable on his new medications that Dr. Bernard asked Jill if she could handle Charles at home. Jill was very open to the idea, mainly because she knew she could count on Charles' parents for the next two months. Moreover, when vacation started, she would have more time to dedicate to Charles at home and continue her analyses of his brain images. There was an issue, however; Charles could not be in freedom. The only reason he was out of jail was because Dr. Bernard was keeping him in the psychiatric ward.

The young man from the alley that survived Charles' attack was still in the rehabilitation hospital with paralysis of one side of his body and unable to remember much about his fight with Charles. His family had pressed charges against Charles accusing him of murder and battering of their son to a point that the boy was destroyed for life. They wanted Charles in jail and a major sum in money to support their son's care for life and money to cover for his possible loss of earnings throughout life.

The hospital records showed that the young man was under drugs; moreover, he had episodes of withdrawal diagnosed during the period he was in rehabilitation. Dr. Bernard and Dr. Hillary were working with the police to explain that Charles acted in self-defense and that he was attacked by the two fellows in the dark alley. Both were students with very poor grades in contrast to Charles' outstanding academic and sports achievements. Against Charles was his history of violence in his police file. These registered episodes of violence had led the judge to conclude that Charles was a danger to society. He ruled that Charles should be kept in a psychiatric hospital until the final trial.

Dr. Hillary suggested that Charles should return to his studies because the psychiatric ward of the university hospital was in the same building of the laboratory he was working. Charles could be escorted to the laboratory and back to the ward at the end of his working hours.

Jill was encouraged by Dr. Hillary's suggestion. She needed, however, continuous help from Charles' parents to keep him company during the period he would be working in the laboratory. Charles' thesis advisor was open to try any arrangement to have him back to work. He had learned to like and admire Charles for his dedication and intelligence. He also felt very comfortable with Charles returning to work because he had experienced his kindness during the two years that he observed Charles at work.

Mr. Morales was a full professor of mathematics at the university in San Diego decided to ask for one year of sabbatical and went to study calculations at UCLA related to nanotechnology. This way he started working in the same laboratory Charles was developing his electrodes and recording devices. Charles' advisor was delighted to have such a competent mathematician in his laboratory supporting his and Charles' work. During the next year of Charles' and Jill's life the progress in their research was outstanding.

Although Greg, in his 6 months of research work, was not able to find differences in the two image datasets from Charles' brain, he was able to organize the images for comparison. His first three months of work, while Jill was finishing her quarter and Charles was recovering, consisted of learning the computer software, transfer of data, and fusion of images. Dr. Hillary's laboratory physicists were extremely helpful to him. When Jill's vacation started, she joined Greg in data analysis. Their work, although productive, was without major breakthroughs. It was however a solid buildup of voxel by voxel comparison of images. They did not have the chance to magnify their comparisons, but were able to complete voxel by voxel matching of Fred's and Charles' images. Greg had to return to the clinical service, leaving Jill alone in her studies for the next 6 months.

During this period, Randy came from San Diego every weekend with Jill's parents. The two families, Charles' and Jill's, became so close that happiness was flowing at very high level between them. They were very hopeful that the final trial on the accusations against Charles would rule for his complete freedom. The trial was scheduled for the last month of Jill's one year research break. Randy was now 3 years old. He had not had any episode of seizures since Jill's mother understood the need of giving him the medications religiously.

Dr. Hillary had introduced Jill to his businessman friend. He decided to support Jill, and cover her expenses while she finished medical school. He gave her a stipend in the form of scholarship. The money was transferred to the university accounts as a donation to Dr. Hillary's research. Dr. Hillary would then pay Jill as a researcher in his laboratory. Life was again smiling on the young couple, their parents, and Randy.

Chapter 43
Physicists

Dr. Hillary called Jill and his physicists for a meeting. Greg was also present because he was an integral part of the research, although he had no time to dedicate to data analyses at this time. He was completely swamped in clinical work for his fourth year of residence. His clinical obligations would not leave time for him to work or think scientifically. He had however, great surgical capabilities. He was now dedicated to develop the surgical technique with Dr. Hillary and was less involved in the targeting portion of the procedure to control aggressive behavior. His admiration for Jill's intelligence had increased since he worked closely with her during those 3 months they overlapped during their research time.

The physicists liked and respected Greg, but they were more impressed with the brightness and dedication that Jill had demonstrated during the 10 months they had opportunity to work with her. They were completely amazed with the data set she had made available for their studies. The problem was that the number of voxels to be compared was so overwhelming that until now they were not able to identify a single difference between the resting and aggressive imaging datasets.

Dr. Hillary started the meeting brainstorming. Ideas were collected at random, until Greg suggested that they should direct their comparisons to specific areas of the brain already known to be related to aggressive behavior, instead of throwing the net in a fishing expedition at an ocean of voxels. Dr. Hillary asked him to suggest the areas he thought would be likely to yield interesting findings. Greg immediately pointed out the medial portions of the temporal lobes, the cingulated giri and the base of the frontal lobes. He had been studying for his neurosurgical boards and read that these areas were commonly affected after head injury, many times leading patients to become aggressive during the period of recovery.

Jill, on the other hand, was interested in studying the hypothalamus. She was interested on this structure for several reasons. The main pressing one was that she knew it in detail because of her studies on hamartomas. She became obsessed about the hypothalamus after she learned that Randy could have hypothalamic problems because of his hamartoma. The second but less pressing reason was that she was led to think that the sympathetic region of the hypothalamus was deeply affected during the aggressive behavior. The increase in blood pressure and the pupillary dilation she had observed on Fred and Charles at the time of rage onset were very suggestive of a focal discharge from the hypothalamus. She just needed to localize precisely in this structure where the discharge was occurring.

She asked Dr. Hillary what he thought about concentrating her efforts in a one-centimeter cubic region encompassing the basal portion of the hypothalamus. The very region were Randy's hamartoma was attached. She had observed Randy's impatient behavior and talked with her mother-in-law regarding it. She said that Randy's behavior was in many ways similar to Charles' behavior when he was a toddler. Dr. Hillary felt this observation to be interesting. He didn't have any great idea beyond the ones that Greg and Jill had suggested. However, he was very much in agreement with Jill's rationale.

The physicists were also very encouraged to study a one-centimeter cubic region. They felt they could help Jill compare voxel by voxel in that small volume in both, Fred's and Charles' hypothalamus in less than one month. Dr. Hillary gave the go-ahead to them and suggested that if they failed, they should follow Greg's idea. All left the meeting full of hope.

Chapter 44
Breakthrough

Jill focused all her attention on her research. She stopped spending time daily with Charles in the ward. She started working at 6:30 AM together with the physicists and finished late at night. Her dedication was so impressive that the physicists could not help but do their best to keep her company throughout her working hours. It was 11 PM on a Saturday night; she was alone and totally immersed in Charles' brain images when she first saw an encouraging difference between two voxels. It was the first time she saw brain areas of specific epinephrine up take. It was in the length of the fasciculum of Vicq D'Azyr, a group of neural fibers participating in the connection of the limbic system. A portion of the brain with cells related to primitive behavior. She brought the atlas and fused the image immediately to confirm the location. She built up a volume of voxels progressing one by one and comparing the new volume built in each image.

After adding the voxels surrounding the first finding over a period of approximately one hour of computer manipulation, she defined a volume of two cubic millimeters that was completely different in the two images. As she added more voxels the addition just decreased the difference in uptake in the two images, suggesting that she was leaving the volume of interest.

She immediately brought Fred's images up and started to compare voxels in the region of his hypothalamus analogous to Charles' fasciculum of Vicq D'Azyr. As she expected, the difference was found, here however only in a volume of less than 1 mm. She had to magnify the image at least 10 times to start to notice the difference in voxels. She understood then why she had been so unsuccessful over the past three years on identifying differences on epinephrine up take in Fred's images. She had never magnified his images this much. Moreover, she was never guided by the findings she identified in Charles' images. She was so excited that she called Dr. Hillary at 3 AM.

"Dr. Hillary, sorry to wake you up, but I have to share this with someone. You are the only person who will fully understand what I just saw."

"Don't worry, this is the time I routinely wake up, I don't know why, I usually fall sleep again. What is up?"

"I identified the area in the hypothalamus I was looking for. It is in the same area that I imagined based on Randy's scan. This small area of radioactive epinephrine uptake is in the base of the hypothalamus, where the fasciculum of Vicq D'Azyr passes. I matched this area with the atlas software. This area is identifiable in both; Charles' and Fred's raging brain and bilaterally, but it is not identified in the images of their brains in normal state. The anatomic position is analogous in both species."

"Amazing! It measures 2 cubic millimeters in Charles' brain and 0.5 cubic millimeters in Fred's, actually it is disproportionably larger in Fred's brain. It is only 4 times smaller in Fred's brain when in reality Fred's entire brain is actually 15 times smaller than that of Charles. I cannot understand why? Is it because the monkey's brain is more primitive than the human's brain; therefore, having this area more prominent in monkeys? Would this disproportion explain their savage behavior?"

"Eureka, girl! You are thinking too much and asking too many questions, we can discuss this proportionality business later. Now you need to go tell Charles what you saw and celebrate it with him. The rest of us will celebrate this at a more decent hour. Goodnight!"

Chapter 45
Should She?

Jill buzzed the nurse on call at the door of the psychiatric ward where dangerous patients were lodged. The nurse received her surprised, Jill had not been going there at night, she was over worked; any minute she had she would go home to rest, spend time with Randy and crash in bed. Jill's and Charles' relationship had changed over those years since the incident in the alley. She was always treating him like a patient, a dependent and needy person. She needed her old Charles. She needed to share with him that most important finding for her and Charles.
Hopefully, she would capture back their past passion. She asked the nurse if she could have some privacy with Charles. The nurse smiled at her. She was a mature nurse who had spent her professional life in the psychiatric ward; she had lived this situation with other patients.

Charles had a private room in the ward. He gained the nurses' sympathy because of his exemplary behavior, now for more than one year. They also understood that he needed a private place to study. Jill entered the room, Charles was sleeping. She undressed herself completely and lay down beside him. He didn't wake up. She started kissing his ear gently and tried to wake him with small bites on his earlobe. He smiled in his sleep and finally opened his eyes. She insisted on trying to sexually arouse him, gently and patiently, until she noticed tears running from his eyes.

"Charlie, I am so happy, I came here to tell you that I found the site in your brain that we will implant the device you have almost ready. I have my part ready," she said, kneeling in bed at his side and looking at him from above with her big dark eyes.

Tears kept on running through his face and he said, "You are so beautiful," and closed his eyes, sobbing.

"Charlie, I love you, we are finally finding the solution for our problem. All will be fine; I will be always with you."

He just cried and cried and cried. She too cried, dressed and left the room.

The nurse looked at her with an approving smile while she walked through the nursing station and mumbled thanks.

It was already 5 AM. She walked to the computer laboratory and started again working on the computer terminal. She wanted to see again those voxels, confirm that she was correct. She didn't want to think about what just happened between her and Charles. She assumed that was the medication that was depressing him and hoped that all would settle down when Charles' hypothalamus was implanted with a smart stimulation device. There was plenty of data in the scientific literature showing that electrical stimulation of the hypothalamus can lead to sustained sexual arousal and intercourse among primates. She thought superficially about this, smiled and dove into her brain imaging world.

Greg showed up one hour later in the laboratory, he was on call that night and had just finished rounds. He usually passed by the laboratory after he finished his work just to organize his thoughts on his research before he went home. He was surprised to find Jill there. She usually would appear at the laboratory around 6:30 AM, when he was already leaving.

"Wow, you are working a storm, a too-tired brain will not be very creative. You will miss important findings in your analyses." He gave her his large smile.

"I found it, Greg, I found it! There is an area of epinephrine uptake in these images. It matches Fred's and Charles' locations. Both are in analogous bilateral areas in the base of the hypothalamus."

"You are dreaming, Jill. You are just too tired. I scrutinized these brains for six months. Nothing is there. I gave up. You need to move on!"

"No, I am really excited with this finding. Come here, let me show you. There is this new magnification software package we received last week that is amazing. I identified two voxels in Charles' brain and one voxel in Fred's brain."

Greg didn't believe it, but as Jill had exhibited great intellectual prowess, he approached the workstation to see what she was trying to show. The whole screen was occupied by minute squares. It looked like a TV set that is not working, just that there was no movement. He could not see any different colors in the squares, except for two squares in the center of the screen that were slightly darker.

"Jill, you are not trying to tell me that those two little squares are in the hypothalamus, are you? I saw plenty of squares like these when I analyzed this data and never could correlate them to anything."

"Look at this," said Jill. She decreased progressively the magnification factor of the image keeping the cursor over the squares. Sure enough, the cursor rested just in the base of the hypothalamus. Then she flipped to Fred's brain and repeated the same demonstration. Bingo! It lay precisely in the base of Fred's hypothalamus.

"Now, look at this," said Jill. She placed the cursor over the same site in another image of Charles' brain and magnified. "You see, nothing is here." "This is Charles' brain without the rage onset. The same is observed in Fred's brain at rest."

"Uhhhh," he mumbled. She looked at him and smiled. He kissed her over that smile. He was so close to her that he couldn't resist. He had been attracted to her for so long; there she was happy, pretty and with those big black intelligent eyes. He kissed and held her with his tight embrace. She didn't react; she actually accepted his kiss as he ran his hand down her back. She kissed him back and embraced him tightly. He was on his scrubs, and she could see his chest and felt him. She slid her hands under his shirt and felt his strong muscles in his back. He took his shirt off and rested her head on his chest. She accepted this familiar gesture. As she felt him more, she started to remember Charles' chest that first night in Westwood. She pulled back and lowered her head. Greg brought her tight, but she resisted.

"Greg, I cannot. He is sick in the ward upstairs. I cannot do this; it is not right. I am going to see Randy."

"We need to get together later. It is not fair that you don't have a life. Do you think you will ever accomplish to take this guy out of this ward? He has killed someone. Again, you are dreaming. When you finally develop this treatment, your years will be gone. I can make you happy now, today."

"Wow, that was one nasty remark! The other times you were insensitive, you acted naively. This was a plain-mean thing to say. I will accomplish what I set myself out to do. I may not end up with Charlie because he has a mind of his own. He may change his mind regarding me, but it will not be because I messed up. Forget about anything between us. Now, I am too tired and confused. I am so happy with tonight's finding and too frustrated with Charles' situation. Now I am flabbergasted by your remark. I need to talk with a reasonable person and discuss all this."

"You are not telling me that you will ask advice from Dr. Hillary about us, are you?"

"No, I don't think he would understand and would be very upset with you. It will be bad for me also. We will have to work together for a long time; it would be awkward for all of us. Well, let me go!"

Chapter 46
Awful

She ran to Charles' ward. She arrived there, sobbing. She felt guilty and awful. How could she? As she entered the ward, she saw Mildred, the older night shift nurse, getting ready to leave. Mildred noticed that she was distressed and asked what was going on. Jill felt secure and told her that she had done something awful.

"You were elated with happiness few hours ago. Do you need to talk? Let's go to the cafeteria, I was planning to have breakfast anyway. Charles is still asleep, last night he was a little agitated with one of the inmates harassing him. I gave him an extra dose of his medication. Dr. Bernard had prescribed provision for us to do so if he became agitated. We are all so afraid that he comes up with a recurrence of that terrible violence mounted with depression."

"So, that is why he barely participated in a conversation with me last night. I feel awful," said Jill.

"If this is why you are so sad, don't worry, tomorrow night you come again. I will withhold his medication for you."

"Mildred, it is not that. It is that while I was working a little more in the laboratory, Greg the handsome resident came by and…"

"Did you have a good time? I noticed on your face that you needed Charlie when you came last night. You were so happy; you had to share it with someone. If he was not available, a 'toy-boy' is an option."

"Please don't talk like this, nothing happened more than my desire for him and a kiss. I came to my senses and came back to the ward because I felt so guilty that I could not go home without seeing Charles."

"Don't make a big drama out of it, what happens in the hospital stays in the hospital, but the whole hospital knows! Well, it stays in the hospital most of the time. Don't feel so bad, Greg is handsome, you are young and healthy, you and Charles have not had a chance for a long time. It is natural to be attracted to someone, don't be so hard on yourself."

"Don't tell me that the whole hospital will know about this."

"Nothing will come out of my mouth and Greg will not tell. Guys never tell when they don't get their way; it is against their pride, especially a famous stud such as Greg. If you don't tell anybody, I believe it will die here!"

"Thanks, this is reassuring," Jill said.

"Just keep a lid on everything and move on with your life. You need all you have to take your Charles out of here, don't waste time and energy on a cheap love affair. Greg is famous among the nurses. He is not as good as he looks, you didn't miss much. Now go home and rest."

"Thanks, I owe you for this pep talk."

"Tonight, I will be here, come for a chat and for your husband if you need."

"I will."

"Congratulations, you are so wholesome. I always will take good care of Charlie for you. What a beautiful love you two have. Another woman would have already forgotten she had a husband."

"Greg still flashes through my head though. He inspires so much more admiration in me than Charlie does. Charlie used to be such an incredible athlete, a great student, and proved to be also a great father. Now he seems so weak and dependent; I don't know if he will be a good role model for Randy, my son."

"He will be always better in the life of your son than any other man. He is his father. His love for him cannot be reproduced by anybody."

"I guess so; I need to get him out of here though."

"Apparently, it all depends on your success as a scientist. You are getting it done. You have gotten past the middle of a long journey. It is natural to feel discouraged and exhausted."

"Sometimes it seems impossible. Greg said it will never happen, but tonight I gave such a huge step finding the proper place in the brain to control his impulsivity."

"Look, don't give up, ever; don't fall into temptations at this time. There are plenty of people to tell what you cannot do, very few wish to help great accomplishments. Come more at night in the ward; you need to spend time with Charlie. You also need someone to talk to. Now that he is working, you two are probably rarely seeing each other. There is no marriage that survives no communication; I have been through three."

"Wow, I guess I can get some advice from you."

"It becomes difficult when such a complicated problem like yours lies between two people. You have a lot in your plate. Sorry, it is 10 AM already, I have to go, count on me for a chat. Reliable friends are better than a good shrink."

"Thank you so much, Mildred, it was a great help, I feel better. Bye."|

"Hello Jill," said Dr. Hillary, entering the cafeteria, as Jill was walking out. "I just changed someone's battery; I need a break. Do you have time for a coffee and a chat? We need to discuss your exciting finding."

"That is all I did today, why not continue?" Jill said.

Chapter 47
Ward-Work Work-Ward

The hospital psychiatric escort brought Charles at 10 AM to the laboratory. His father was already there and very excited.

"Charles, look at this. It is the miniature version of the smart stimulator for you. It measures one by one centimeter. It has a rechargeable battery. You can recharge yourself at bedtime with an electrical pad placed over your head. It has two channels, one for recording, input, and the other for stimulation, output. It has a smart chip to integrate all the information and modulates the level of stimulation needed, depending on impending emotional reactions."

There was no answer from Charles. He sat quietly at his desk and didn't even greet Mr. Morales. When his father asked Charles what was going on, tears ran down his eyes. Mr. Morales also felt a deep feeling of sadness. He was doing all he could to help his son. He had even returned from a professor's level to a student's level in the nanotechnology laboratory in the hope to take Charles from that state. The task was so daunting. He had spent all night in the laboratory working under the microscope, placing the device's circuitry together. He was exhausted and needing some cheering up himself. Even though he had finished the device prototype and was excitedly trying to show it to Charles, he was insecure of its appropriate functioning. Moreover, he had no idea how Dr. Hillary would like the design and whether he would be willing to use it.

After trying to no avail to get Charles' attention, Mr. Morales gave up and invited him for a coffee. Although Charles had no interest in getting out of his chair and again didn't answer, Mr. Morales ushered him to the hospital cafeteria. He hoped that a lively environment would cheer both of them up. Maybe Charles was tired of the ward-work, work-ward routine and needed to see different people.

Chapter 48
Out of Control

Dr. Hillary sat with his coffee; Jill continued with the coffee she had while she was talking with Mildred. They used the same table; it was located in the center of the busy hospital cafeteria. They were both absorbed with their conversation. Jill described the process of finding the voxels of interest. She described the minute location in the hypothalamus where the voxels were located and the amazing correspondence on the location of these voxels when comparing Charles' and Fred's brain images. She again insisted the correspondence of this minute hypothalamic region with the mammillothalamic tract seen in the brain atlas. This location confirmed the presence of this important behavior related region, the fasciculum of Vicq D'Azyr, inside the limbic system. This suggested that indeed the voxels she found were related to triggering Charles' violent fits. She was excited and nonstop talking when she saw Charles walking into the cafeteria with Mr. Morales holding his arm.

Mr. Morales saw Jill waving to them, inviting them to sit at the same table. Mr. Morales walked Charles toward her, sat him besides Jill and went to buy his and Charles' coffee. Charles sat quietly without greeting Dr. Hillary or Jill, even though both of them complimented him enthusiastically.

"Hello! Charles, you look good, it is nice seeing you on an outing. It is great that you are here with us," said Jill, standing up and kissing his cheek.

Charles gave a shy smile and looked at Dr. Hillary. Apparently, he wanted to say something but lowered his head and stayed quiet. Dr. Hillary and Jill continued their conversation.

"Charles, I was describing to Dr. Hillary what I told you last night."

"Do you remember anything?" Dr. Hillary asked worriedly.

Charles made an interrogating face and again did not answer.

"I guess you took too much medication, Charles. Mildred, the nurse, told me this morning that she gave you an extra dose because you were a little agitated last night. Apparently, there was a fellow in the ward bothering you. Do you remember?"

Charles looked at her with the same interrogating face and stood up to leave. Dr. Hillary immediately said, "Wait Charles, your father is just coming with a huge tray of food."

Charles sat down quietly. Mr. Morales arrived with a large tray of breakfast.

"Does anybody want to help me? I spent all night long in the microscope finalizing the nanodevice for you guys to implant in Charles' brain. Are you ready to use it?"

"Exciting, I just defined the site in Charles' brain that should be implanted. Now, it is just a matter of linking all the dots."

"What do you think about all this, Charles?" asked Dr. Hillary.

No answer from Charles, he had just accepted the cup of coffee and was sipping it almost mechanically. He was expressionless. Only Jill's greeting had opened for seconds his face. He was apparently not there with them.

Dr. Hillary was growing worried with Charles' depressive behavior but continued the conversation, since Charles was surrounded by people that loved him. He was out of the ward and laboratory for the first time in about one year.

It was reasonable that he behaved somewhat shy. Dr. Hillary listened attentively as Mr. Morales described the device. He liked the design and actually found it extremely ingenuous. The whole device would fit inside a small drill hole in the skull without any superficial hint that there was a device implanted. No wiring under the skin was necessary. The wires coming from the depth of the brain would terminate in the device. The device was screwed flush with the skull surface. It was perfect for the majority of psychiatric patients wanting to keep their disease private.

They were absorbed with Mr. Morales' description and did not see when Greg entered the cafeteria. He saw the group talking and approached them after he had bought himself a coffee. As he stood up close to Jill to choose a chair, she noticed that Charles' pupils where dilating. She stood to hold back Charles, but it was too late. Charles lifted the table over Dr. Hillary and Mr. Morales and punched Greg's face. At the same time, he punched his belly and wrapped his arm around his neck and started to squeeze tighter and tighter.

Greg had no chance to react. The punch opened a wound in Greg's right brow from where blood was flowing over his face. Charles' violent movements spilled blood and coffee everywhere. When Dr. Hillary and Mr. Morales finally stood up, Greg's body was already limp in Charles' arms.

Dr. Hillary jumped over Charles and wrapped his arms around his neck. Charles was however strong and fought back, pushing Dr. Hillary away, who again fell to the floor. Charles proceeded to kick Greg's body that was motionless on the floor. Dr. Hillary stood up and again tried to wrap his arms around Charles' neck. Mr. Morales, now close enough, was able to embrace Charles and hold his arms. Charles was able to free himself from them and started running to the door.

At this point, two security guards were entering the cafeteria. They had been called to the scene. When they saw Charles covered by blood, they ran toward him. Charles knocked the first one down with a punch in his head and tried to escape through the door. The second security pulled his gun and shot Charles' leg. He fell down, stood up again, and continued running. Now the two securities ran after him and caught him in the corridor and knocked him unconscious. They took him to the emergency room. Blood was gushing from his leg.

Greg arrived in the emergency room unconscious. His neck was immediately stabilized by the doctors. The blood covering his face was coming from a small wound in his brow; however, an artery had been severed. The bleeding was promptly controlled with a simple staple. He was not breathing on his own. He arrived in the emergency room under artificial ventilation with an ambo bag. A tube was placed in his trachea, and he was placed on mechanical ventilation. He was transported to the CT scan room. The scan showed that he had no intracranial bleeding but had a massive brain swelling. He had spent a long time under hypoxia. Charles had held his neck compressed for a long time, cutting blood supply to his brain. The situation was severe. He had also three broken ribs and a huge swelling had begun on his face. One could not recognize him.

Jill, who had followed the paramedics to the emergency room, saw Charles being taken to the operating room for an exploration of the gunshot wound in his thigh. He was moving the leg, a good sign that the bullet that entered his thigh had not severed his sciatic nerve. The bullet had exited his leg without causing further damage. There was, however, profuse bleeding through the exit wound, that is why they had to take him to the operating room. Most likely they would have to repair an artery.

When Jill saw Greg, she started sobbing uncontrollably. She couldn't believe her eyes. How could this tragedy happen? Was it her fault? Had Charlie perceived somehow that something had happen between her and Greg? Would Greg recover? The tall nurse, her friend in the emergency ward, came and injected a sedative in her vein. She placed her in one of the emergency private rooms and let her sleep.

Chapter 49
Guilt

Charles returned from surgery on artificial breathing. Although he had received an epidural anesthesia to allow surgery and analgesia for his leg, he was too agitated to be maintained awake. The surgery in his leg was simple. There was rupture of a small artery and no lesion of major nerves in the leg. He would recover without difficulty from the gunshot wound. Would he recover as fast from his depression and aggressive state? Dr. Hillary and Dr. Bernard decided to maintain him under heavy sedation for the following 2 days in the intensive care unit. He would be transferred to his room in the dangerous patients' psychiatric ward if he could be maintained under mild sedation.

Jill woke up 36 hours later. She was brought home by Mr. Morales who was very depressed. When they arrived home, he cooked a meal and sat for dinner with Jill. He started saying: "Jill, I have to apologize. It was a huge mistake to take Charles to the cafeteria."

"Don't blame yourself. How could you know?"

"It was poor judgment; I was too tired after a night of work to think clearly. Charles was not his normal self. He was not answering my questions and showed no excitement for the fact I finished putting his device together. I should have brought him back to the ward and gone home to rest. Instead, I decided to play doctor trying to cheer him up taking him to the cafeteria. I should know by now that when Charles is depressed, there is no easy fix."

"You haven't slept since yesterday. You are too tired. Stop thinking like this and go to bed. Tomorrow you will have a new outlook on all this. I feel well after all these hours of sleep. I will go to the hospital to visit Charles and see how Greg is. I heard they are both in the same intensive care unit."

"Why don't you go tomorrow? It is late for you to go alone, Jill."

"No, I am used to going to the hospital at this hour. It is also a good time to get hold of Dr. Hillary. He usually finishes his surgeries by 6 PM, does his patient rounds, and spends a half-hour in the cafeteria talking with the residents before going home. I will meet him in the cafeteria to discuss what we will do for Charles and ask about Greg before I visit them."

"You know what you are doing. I will call the ladies in San Diego to ask about Randy. I will not tell them anything that transpired here as yet. I will wait for you to return. We can call them tomorrow. There is nothing they can do from there to help the situation here."

"Thanks Dad, you have a good rest."

"You are welcome, Jill, don't work too hard, you also need rest."

"As I see it, I have to complete the analysis of the site of implant as soon as possible. The only solution for all this matter in my mind is surgery for Charles. We let it go too far."

"Jill, we did all we could to help Charles," Mr. Morales said.

"I don't know if Greg is damaged for life. I hope not. It will be the end of any possibility for Charles' freedom if he does not recover. His chances of freedom are very slim as it is. Goodnight!"

Chapter 50
Outlook

Jill entered the cafeteria.

"Dr. Hillary, I knew I would find you here in the cafeteria. We need to talk. There is so much on my mind that I don't believe I can go home and sleep without this conversation with you. I know that you must be exhausted, but you are the only person that can help me to understand the whole picture. We also need to come up with a plan of action for Charles' situation. The way I see it, surgery is the only way out. What do you think?"

"Surgery is a must; I just don't know if it is a way out. Depending on how Greg recovers, the situation for Charles can be terrible. I don't want to alarm you, but realistically, I doubt that any judge will let Charles free after his actions resulting in one person dead and two young men destroyed for life. The other two guys were on drugs and all evidence suggests that they attacked Charles. This time there were hundreds of witnesses in that cafeteria seeing Charles deliberately attacking and violently destroying Greg's life without any provocation. It will be hard to absolve him from this one."

"I don't know if I can myself, even if surgery works. I would not trust to leave him in society at this point. Many years of observation with him on brain stimulation therapy will be necessary to prove it is safe to release him from a psychiatric unit."

"What I dreaded my whole life finally happened," Jill said with tears in her eyes.

"I do think, however, that we must offer him surgery to improve his quality of life and make him a productive person. He can work on his scientific projects and developments of devices. He can serve as a test for his own invention, earn a living, and help you raise Randy. If his device works, he will be a rich man, cashing in royalties from his invention."

"I agree with all that you are saying. This is why I am here tonight. I want to talk with you and return to the laboratory to finalize the characterization of the hypothalamic region to implant the recording and stimulation electrode. Mr. Morales is confident that the device will work."

"OK Jill, continue working to ascertain the proper site of implantation. However, we will have to wait for complete healing of the wound in Charles' leg before proceeding with surgery. It would be a too high risk of infection of the device if we proceed with surgery while he has an open and possibly infected would. Also, we need some time to line up all that is necessary."

"I understand. I will be working in the organization of the procedure under your orientation. Thanks for still being willing to help."

"You are always welcome, Jill."

"What about Greg, Dr. Hillary?"

"He does not look good. His brain is very swollen. We had to install an intracranial pressure monitor to manage his high intracranial pressure. He is on hyperventilation and high doses of medication to decrease the pressure. You know, high intracranial pressure compromises the blood supply to the brain with consequent death of cells, disturbing his full recovery."

"The reality is that it has been very hard to control his intracranial pressure. We may have to perform bilateral decompressive craniotomies, i.e., open large windows in his skull in both sides of his head to provide room for his brain to swell. This will prevent the vital areas of the brain from being squeezed in the enclosed skull space, what would lead to death or severe disability."

"Oh no!"

Chapter 51
Vigil

Greg's recovery was slow, 7 weeks in the intensive care unit was necessary to wean him off a ventilator and transfer him to the step-down unit in preparation for a regular ward bed. He was discharged from the ICU with a tracheotomy and a gastrostomy. He had fecal and urinary incontinence. He was in a vigil coma. He would look in all directions but would not interact with the environment. Hope for complete recovery and return to the neurosurgery training was slim.

He finally left the hospital 3 months after he was a victim of Charles' assault. He was transferred to a rehabilitation center, still in vigil coma. His tracheotomy tube had been removed; however, he was still dependent on his gastric tube for food intake. He did not show any signs of interaction with the environment. He still needed a urinary catheter and diapers. His mother was with him all times. His father did not accept the reality of the matter. Greg was their only son.

Although his mother, a pediatrician, was depressed and had stop working to be with him, his father, a lawyer, was charged with anger against Charles. He had already pressed criminal charges and wanted to see Charles locked up for life. One could understand his feelings; his only son had been seriously injured without a good reason. He was at work; he was bright and a good person. Nobody knew of his inclinations for Jill, Charles' wife. Only Jill, not even Charles could understand well what happened. Charles instincts had felt something wrong between Jill and Greg. Was the primitive part of Charles' brain strongly linked to his feelings of fear to lose Jill? Are instincts sharper at the savage level of beings? Charles had shown that this theory had merit.

Why do savage animals know to run before the danger is clear and present? Why do fights in the animal kingdom happen out of pure instinctive grounds, only threat? Charles was threatened by Greg's proximity to Jill. He knew to be weaker and at a position of eminent loss. He attacked, taking the advantage of surprise, which is common in the animal kingdom. He was successful. He destroyed the presumptive enemy. He would be victorious in the animal kingdom, but not under human laws. He was now defenseless to be committed to incarceration for life, at minimum in a psychiatric institution.

The same human laws that prevented Charles from having the surgical procedure that could avoid the chain of tragedies that happen in his life would be the ones to condemn him to a life in prison, away from his child and his wife. Laws developed in reaction to mistakes of doctors performing surgery indiscriminately, without sound indication, abusing the doctor's privilege of helping people in their most vulnerable period of their lives, exclusively for greed and vanity. Should Charles, Jill, Randy and his grandparents, Greg and his family pay for the errors of doctors in the past?

Jill finally understood why Dr. Hillary had the conversation with her and Charles about the past errors of doctors, at the time called psychosurgeons. She understood all the depth, the beauty, and the responsibility of having the talent and the right to care for people with diseases.

Chapter 52
Device

Mr. Morales took his prototype stimulator to a small company developing sensing neurological devices in Southern California. This small company was dedicated to developing sensory devices, visual devices with interaction directly with the cerebral cortex, and less specialized sensations such as touch and pain in extremities. He posed to the company the challenge of commercializing the hypothalamic stimulator. He would give the company the prototype with all of Charles' and his ideas to have a device constructed in a record time to implant in Charles.

The family was desperate; Charles was under heavy sedation since the episode in the cafeteria. Six months had already passed and whenever he was allowed to wake up from the sedation, he would become violent. The only hope was an implant of an effective device in the very site discovered by Jill.

Using Charles' and Mr. Morales' circuitry, a commercially acceptable device was developed by the company. The owner of the company did it without claiming property rights on the device. He understood the effort that the family had placed on its development, making it strictly for Charles' surgery. The subject was anyway too controversial for a small company to risk its reputation with investors. Mr. Morales signed a contract of first and exclusive distribution by the company if Charles improved and the device became approved.

Dr. Hillary, Dr. Mallory, and Dr. Larsson took it upon themselves to implant the first device in a wild monkey. These experienced professional scientists applied all their talent to make the experiment successful. The surgery went well, and they proved that the animal was made docile when the device was on. This docility would disappear if the device was turned off with a remote control. The animal's desire to attack was curbed by an automatic mechanism of recognition of firing of cells in the hypothalamus, in the very site described by Jill. They returned the animal to the colony with the stimulating device off. They observed the complete adaptation of the animal to his usual environment.

If proper laws allowed the use of this device in carefully selected patients, the impact of Jill's and Charles' accomplishment would be worthy of a Nobel Prize, for the same reason Egas Moniz received the Nobel Prize of Medicine in 1949 for the discovery of the effects of lobotomy on humans. Millions of people would benefit, not only the patients committed to life without freedom, but also their families and society at large, violent crimes could be somewhat controlled, or at least have their incidence decrease. Their device would avoid the terrible side-effects of the infamous lobotomy, or infamous treatments, such as the psychological modification portrayed in the controversial novel of Anthony Burgess, *A Clockwork Orange*. Moreover, it would also avoid the undesirable side-effects of systemic pharmacological solutions.

Chapter 53
Resident

Jill's mechanism of defense was work. She finished her thesis, earned her doctorate in behavioral imaging, and proved that the site she had isolated in the hypothalamus was indeed the site first activated in preparation for a violent attack. Her research reports were accepted for publication in the most competitive scientific journals; she received several young investigator awards and earned national and international recognition for her expertise. She was invited and accepted the opportunity to train in neurosurgery at UCLA. Dr. Hillary proposed her acceptance, ironically in the slot left vacant by the unfortunate Greg.

Jill started residence when Randy was 7 years old. Seven years were taken by her medical school, doctorate degree and all the tragedy surrounding her life. Charles was still under heavy sedation when she was on call for the whole hospital covering neurosurgery. She visited him every night she was on call. She invariably left the visits with tears in her eyes. She brought Randy to see his dad every weekend. She wanted Randy to know that he didn't have a father at home because his father, a great man, athlete, and scientist was sick. She always told her son, "As soon as Mom is better trained, she will help your father wake up. I am sure he will teach you to play soccer." Randy knew of his father's past success as an athlete, Mr. Morales had shown his grandson all the videos of the glorious moments of his father's life. Randy was growing up proud of his father.

Soon after she started her residency, Jill received a letter in her mailbox. It was the permission for the implant of the device in Charles' brain. She had applied to the human subject committee of the university for a Compassionate Permission for the implant. She paged Dr. Hillary immediately with the good news. Two weeks later on a Saturday when Jill and Dr. Hillary were off duty, they implanted the device in Charles' skull with the wire in his hypothalamus. The device was set to be controlled on demand by Charles' brain violent stimulus.

Charles was sent to the recovery room still with the respiratory tube in his mouth and under artificial ventilation. Dr. Hillary instructed the anesthesiologist to let the anesthesia dissipate slowly and let Charles fight the presence of the tube in his mouth. It was expected that as Charles sedation dissipated, he would become violent as he had done for the past 6 months in the Psychiatry ward. This would trigger the stimulation device that in turn would tame his violent instinct.

Jill was anxious to see the success of the operation. The surgery had lasted 4 hours from the time that the MRI for localization of the implantation site was done to the last stitch closing the two 3 centimeter incisions in each of Charles' frontal regions. Jill was still not tired. She was used to continuous 24 hours of work when she was on duty in the hospital and with 10 to 12 hours neurosurgical procedures. After a short lunch while Charles was still in heavy sedation in the recovery room, she returned to his bed side and stayed there anxiously. She also could check with a telemetry device the status of the implanted device, on or off. She could therefore know when the device would be turned on automatically.

She waited. Her telemetry programmer detected when the device automatically turned on. Charles opened his eyes and looked at Jill. She saw when his pupils dilated. They immediately returned to normal. A smile came in his face. She kissed his forehead.

Chapter 54
Son

Randy was a sharp student. He had grown to be a handsome, tall, dark hair and big dark eyed boy. He was a gentleman in class, with outstanding grades and was an outstanding son. Jill and Randy were living close to the hospital and his school. They visited Charles every day in his ward. Charles had acquired more freedom since the implant of the device. He no longer needed full-time observation and was allowed to work in the nanotechnology laboratory. He was not depressed and appreciated spending hours talking with Randy. During the weekends they played soccer in the university sports complex. They became very close friends; Randy had an affinity for soccer. As his father, he played in the school team as a center forward.

Jill was on call every other day in the neurosurgical team. One afternoon, she was called to the emergency room to see a child arriving comatose after a head trauma. It was a blond 7-year-old boy with dilated pupils and not responding to any stimulation. The story told was that he got into a fight at school and was pushed violently hitting his head on the cement floor less than 30 minutes before his arrival in the emergency ward. He was initially awake immediately after the fall, but drifted out of consciousness as he was being transported to the hospital.

She took him immediately to the operating room performed a portable tomography and drained the large blood clot that was compressing his brain. She saved the boys' life. He was on the way to recovery without any neurological damage. He was transported and attended promptly by a competent professional.

She learned soon, after the surgery, that Randy had pushed the boy during a basketball match at school, after the boy fouled on him. She immediately sent a text message to Dr. Hillary: "It is time to treat Randy's hamartoma. No delays, please!"

Postscript

This science-fiction novel questions the prohibition of psychosurgery present in the majority of America's states and several countries in the world. It focuses on endearing love and life challenges for the youth in this century; uncontrolled aggressive behavior is discussed. The author is an experienced functional neurosurgeon and a emeritus professor of neurosurgery at the University of California in Los Angeles. He has edited several books describing minimally invasive therapies of the brain. His experience with psychosurgery dates to his neurosurgical training in Brazil 20 years ago, where he saw the impressive results of surgery for aggressive behavior.

He also acquired further experience while working in Sweden where psychosurgery continued to be performed throughout the end of the last century. Modern techniques of brain imaging, stereotactic brain surgery, and pacemakers for the brain call for a revisit to psychosurgery. The current realization of the psychiatric community that the drugs available fail to help approximately 15% of patients with severe psychiatric diseases brings this subject into light.

The author touches on the emotional, legal, ethical, and medical issues of psychosurgery. A complete discussion of the subject from the experimental laboratory to the surgery on humans is presented with attention to modern neuroscience and brain mapping.

Suggested Reading

1. *Psychosurgery* (1972) edited by Edward Hitchcock, Lauri Laitinen, Kjeld Vaernet, Springfield, Illinois, USA.

2. Redfield, J.K. (1993) *Touched with Fire. Maniac-Depressive Illness and the Artistic Temperament*, New York: The Free Press.

3. Friedman, R.A., M.D. (2006) 'Violence and mental illness: how strong is the link?', *New England Journal of Medicine*, 355.

4. Furtado, V. (2006) 'Psychiatrists face a small but real risk from seriously ill patients', *BMJ*, 333:1112.

5. Hauptman, J.S., De Salles, A.A.F., Espinoza, R., Sedrak, M. and Ishida, W. (2008) 'Potential surgical targets for deep brain stimulation in treatment-resistant depression', *Neurosurg Focus*, 25(1):E3.Sedrak, M., Gorgulho, A., De Salles, A., Frew, A., Behnke, E., Ishida, W., Klochov, T. and Malkasian, D. (2008) 'The role of modern imaging modalities on deep brain stimulation targeting for mental illness', *Acta Neurochir*, **101**:3–7.

6. Neurosurgical Treatments of Psychiatric Disorders Surgery (2015), edited by Bomin Sun, Antonio de Salles, Springer.

7. NeuroRadiosurgery: Case Review Atlas Osama Abdelaziz and Antonio De Salles (2023), Springer.